BEAST OF WONDER

BEAST OF WONDER

LILITH SAINTCROW

For N. D., as always.

Venenum in poculus aureum.

MUNDI REGNUM

1

———

A BLONDE STEWARDESS, HER HAIRSPRAY-TEASED HEAD COCKED at an impossible, lolling angle, smiled with blood-threaded teeth as a pilot's disembodied voice floated through an aluminum tube. *Ladies and gentlemen...ladies and gentlemen...* Outside small thick windows, hungry grey air screamed. Light and dark revolved, crunch-thumping as carryons, magazines, purses, and other daily objects became missiles tumbling through space, flickering through eyelid-flutter strobes. Right and left changed places, and a woman in the red skirt and brown coat held her seat arms with white knuckles, staring at the stewardess in the jumpseat. Trim, uniformed arms and legs flopped like a doll's; the blond stewardess gazed with wide, horrified, glazed blue eyes and that crimson-laced, jolly rictus.

One last terrific jolt raced through a winged tube that had been meant to carry three hundred people to Cincinnati. Then the windows cracked, and the roaring swallowed every soul on board.

It was over.

But that was just the beginning.

2

———————

THUMP-CLATTER, CLATTER-THUMP. A SILVERMETAL SNAKE carried suitcases on its back, tags fluttering from greasy plastic and nylon handles.

People heaved luggage from the snake's back, banging corners and wheels on flat metal plate-scales. The crowd paid no attention to the black-haired woman in a red skirt, assuming she was a fellow passenger. Her brown canvas jacket was almost longer than her skirt; her sweater, underneath, was well-worn cashmere. Her knees were pale and taut, one marred by the white scar of a long-healed wound, and her low black heels had diamanté buckles. Long black hair, slightly mussed, wasn't anything out of the ordinary. She was pale, but everyone under airport fluorescents looks rumpled and slightly sick; frizzled or limp hair and cheese-colored cheeks are normal and ignorable.

The last suitcase was a battered brown leather one without wheels, hefted by an elderly black man with a shock of tightly kinked grey hair. He glanced uneasily at the woman as he heaved his burden free. "Yours didn't come?"

Disembodied female voices floated above them, calling a

garbled name to a courtesy phone, and another flight's luggage was about to start on another carousel. The woman's blue gaze filled with sudden consciousness, a wounded bird beating against the bars of a just-discovered cage.

"It's all right." The man stood a decent distance away, practiced after a lifetime of carefully weighing space. "You just go on over there." He pointed with one gnarled hand, the cuff of his corduroy suit jacket worn shiny. "See that window? They'll take your name and get you yo' stuff."

Her mouth opened a little, chapped lips cracking slightly. "Thanks," she husked, like she hadn't spoken for a long time. You got dried out on airplanes, with all the canned air blowing. She turned, lifting one limp hand to shade her eyes, and gazed at the window he'd pointed at.

It was shut with a rolling metal screen, its bars glittering. A yellowed paper sign flapped from a tab of tape, probably *back in five minutes*. There was no use in protesting. The man was already shuffling away, listing under the weight rubbing at his right knee. The set of his thin shoulders said he knew where he was going and would get there in his own due time, thank you and good day.

The blue-eyed woman wormed her hands into her pockets. Her fingertips explored the inner seams. Nothing, not even lint. No pocket in her skirt, no purse strap on her shoulder. Empty. Blank. *Tabula rasa.*

A thought bubbled dimly up inside the cottonwool filling her skull.

What happened?

Her hands were normal, cupped palms and long tapering fingers, a ghost of dark cherry polish on short-bitten nails. No rings. No necklace, no earrings. No wallet. She studied her surroundings—concrete pillars with chipped paint stood sentinel between the baggage carousels, some of the metal snakes moving, others dead and empty. Escalators moved in the distance. Posters clung to the pillars, one tempting weary travelers with a trip to Bali and another exhorting caution with your luggage. *Don't let it out of your sight*, tall yellow letters blared over a blond woman in a trim blue uniform pointing at a pile of brand-new suitcases.

The uniformed woman's blonde updo and white, even smile sent chills up her back, and she hurriedly looked away.

Short-pile nylon carpet with a pattern of interlocking pipes tried to pull her toward glass doors, opening and closing with chewing regularity. She put her head down and hurried past, onto the up escalator simply because there was no downward one.

The bar was a dim cave with a few slumped shadows on stools, television screens bleary alcoholic eyes full of bright dancing commercials. Instead, she found a deserted restroom. A long row of mirrors glowed over a counter pocked with metal sinks and littered with damp twists of used paper towels, and she avoided looking directly into any reflective glass, ducking into the first stall and closing the door. The toilet was clean enough, and even if she could have produced a slight trickle from her bladder the sound would have been lost in the hum of a big open building. An unnecessary wipe, flush, stand—no panties. Was that usual? She felt fine, except for the tightness in her calves from the low heels. Their buckles glittered even in the stall's shadows.

Maybe the attempt at a bodily function had jolted something loose, because *now* she was thinking. The world came back into focus, and she stood with one hand spread against the stall's cold metal door.

First things first, she decided. Her name. What was her name?

She could dredge up no name, no occupation, no status. Nothing but a crimson smile and a deep, patchwork, welling terror before the slow chugging of a silver snake-beast. She stood in the stall for a long time, trying to remember.

And completely, utterly failing.

A bright crisp day on the edge of fall shaded into early evening, stretching shadows a little too purple for afternoon. The bus to downtown was free, so she climbed aboard, smiling nervously at a heavyset driver in an orange vest. He ignored her, banging the door closed with a quick efficient motion, a blue cap pulled low over his eyes and a grizzling of iron-colored stubble on his thick, reddened cheeks. She found an orange plastic seat near a window halfway back, hideously exposed to incurious glances from the few passengers. All of them had suitcases, purses, pockets bulging with identification and detritus. Receipts. Markers of their place in the world.

One, a lean corn-haired young man in a leather jacket, kept glancing at her. She shook her hair down on that side, curtaining her face, and gazed out the dust-filmed window. The bus heaved and chugged onto a clogged freeway. Billboards flashed past—one had a woman with long dark hair, pale beringed hands folded near her throat where a diamond necklace flashed. *Cara Jewelers*, it whispered in heavy calligraphy. *Beauty Everlasting.*

Beauty everlasting had a nice sound to it. She hunched

her shoulders, interlacing her own naked fingers and squeezing hard enough to turn the knuckles pale.

"Hey." It was the young man in the leather jacket, its buckles and rivets gleaming. He'd left his seat and slid into the empty one just behind her. "You okay?"

She nodded, her hair swinging as the bus braked. "Fine." The word was husky, unused, sandpaper in her dry throat.

"You sure? You look a little upset." He had a nice voice, but his elbows were on the back of the seat, and it bothered her. An invasion of her little bubble—the irritation was familiar, and so was the sharp metallic edge of...what? Fear?

Men who put even a fingertip into your space would soon try to claw further in. She remembered *that*, at least.

"I'm fine," she repeated, keeping her chin pointed at the window. "Thanks."

Maybe he believed her. In any case, he settled back as the silver bus jerked away from the stop. It lurched, guzzled, snorted, and crawled along. Concrete towers mounted on either side, rose into spires. More billboards—auto repair, collision lawyers, elect a new mayor.

None of them held any clue. The corn-haired man's gaze rested heavily on the back of her head. If that weight would have jarred her memory, she would have welcomed it. An itch grew under her skin. She longed to be walking, striding purposefully along, somewhere, anywhere. Maybe if she could move for a little while, she'd remember something. Maybe she could go to the police?

The very thought triggered a hot, nasty wave of nausea, turning meat and gristle behind her breastbone into a knot. No, better to just try and figure it out on her own. Breathe deeply and let the acid roiling settle.

Funny, she didn't feel hungry. Just...sickened.

A half-hour later, the bus jolted up a slight rise and

nosed into a berth at a redone transit center full of saplings in concrete boxes. Painted lines and corners were already showing wear, despite the refurbishment. Slim short bushes, their leaves brushed with red and gold, would grow stunted by exhaust and lopped cruelly as soon as their roots tried to crack confinement. The bus's engine died and the driver glared over his shoulder as a half-dozen or so passengers stirred from the lethargy of poverty travel.

She waited until the yellow-haired young man reluctantly slid past her before moving.

Outside, a cool breeze laden with ghost-dry fallen leaves fingered her bare knees and fluttered the hem of her red skirt. She set off for the biggest cluster of strangers, since the young man in the leather jacket had lit a cigarette and was loitering against one side of an orange and white shelter. The driver banged out of his bus and snarled, "No smoking! Cantcha see the sign?"

"Bite me," was Corn-Hair's reply. The young man inhaled quickly, puffed a small cloud of carcinogens.

Her steps quickened. She joined the milling around the schedule board and stared at a map of the city, multicolored arteries and veins spreading, clotting, spreading again. The itching under her skin mounted, demanded movement, so she turned and set off.

The transit center blended into a park full of late-afternoon crowding, gloved and jacketed couples strolling, street musicians strumming or wailing, teenagers loitering, homeless people alert at the prospect of something, anything useful dropped onto pavement. She moved, an anonymous fish in a large pond, as the sun dipped itself in scarlet clouds and slid-sank behind hungrytooth skyscrapers. The park's fountains were dead and dry, turned off for the winter and possibly to discourage the homeless. Oak trees spread painted branches, scattering colorful but dying leaves as the wind freshened. No rain yet meant each falling scrap of leaf was crisp instead of sludge, pounded into powder on the walkways.

She could go back to the airport and sleep there, perhaps. Dusk gathered and deepened in every corner, streetlights began to spark. She paused at the far end of the park, staring at a crosswalk. On the other side a bodega, a tiny pharmacy, and a parking garage took up most of the block, and a neon sign glowed in the bodega's windows. WIRE TRANSFERS HERE, it called into the gloaming, and the stream of walkers dammed itself up underneath, waiting obediently for the signal.

Among them stood a man in a dark suit and hip-length jacket, the end of a wine-red tie fluttering a little as he stared at her. He had short black hair and the high prow of an aggressive nose, and a small, rumpled paper bag hung from his left hand. The itching under her skin crested. A painful thrill ran from scalp to her compressed toes under glittering buckles.

She almost, *almost* turned away.

The light changed; the black-haired man thrust himself forward, swimming across a dry autumn street with long angry strides. Frozen, she watched his progress, her hands lying limp and useless at the ends of her arms.

He planted his thick-soled leather shoes just inside her personal space, and thrust the paper lunchbag at her. "You're late."

3

———

THE BAG WAS WADDED AROUND A YELLOW APPLE WITH A BLUSH of crimson on one cheek. "You're late," he repeated. A heavy ring glinted on his left middle finger, gold and a blue stone. Later, she would see *Protect and Serve* carved around that deep blue glitter, running her fingertips across sharp etching and hard edges.

At that moment, however, she simply backed up, a nervous half-step familiar to women accosted on evening streets. "I'm sorry?" The apology was familiar too, said daily, hourly, whether you meant it or not.

At least she could remember *that*.

"Come on." His shoulders turned, subtly, inviting her along.

Her throat was still dry. "Do you know me?" The breeze freshened, tugging at her clothes and the fringes of her hair.

"Sent to get you. Black hair, blue eyes, red skirt, long..." Here he paused, eyebrows up, "brown jacket, south end of Vanley Park. Right?"

"You could have been watching me." Her caution was

entirely reasonable. How reasonable was it to wake up with empty pockets, staring at a baggage carousel, remembering nothing?

"Your pockets are empty." His lips stretched with the ghost of a real smile at her visible start. "All right? Come on, we're late."

Now it was *we're late*. The buzzing in her middle tugged her forward. She clutched the apple in its crackling brown paper to her chest, abruptly aware of her calves and thighs aching a bit from walking. It would be nice to sit down.

He didn't wait for anything else, just set off down the sidewalk, obviously expecting her to follow. She did, hurrying until she caught up and he slowed down, shortening his strides. After half a block he glanced at her again. "You got a name?"

Oh, God. A question she couldn't answer. Was lying acceptable? Was it a test? The billboards from the bus trip flashed through her head. "Cara," she said, finally. Beauty everlasting.

It would do.

"I'm Evan. Nice to meet you." He didn't offer his hand. Instead, he dug in his jacket pocket and produced a folded-up red bandanna. A series of coughs shook him as he walked, deep, chesty, sick-sounding chuffs. When they finished, he folded the bandanna again and returned it to its home. "How do you know the old woman?"

Old woman? Maybe it was another test. "I don't think I do," she said, slowly.

"Yeah, well, she said you'd be here, so whatever. You gonna eat? Figured you'd be hungry."

She was still holding the apple. *I'm not hungry.* But it was...impolite, maybe, to refuse? So she took a bite. *Cara. I'm*

Cara. The world dropped into sharp focus with a jolt. Maybe it was her name, maybe it wasn't, but it *felt* right.

Crisp, cool, and only half sweet, the apple resisted her teeth. It felt good to chew, and good to have a name and a destination. Someone expected her, at least. She could piece together the rest of it, bit by bit.

Their destination was a wide brown boat of an ancient gas-guzzling Chevy parked half in an alley, in defiance of the NO PARKING sign under a tangle of graffiti. She had to turn sideways to wriggle in on the passenger side, and the interior smelled of stale cigarette smoke and old aftershave. The man, running a hand over his rasping black buzzcut, dropped into the driver's seat; a plastic tag with a number and barcode on it swung from the rearview. LE PARKING PERMIT, it shouted.

It confused her for a moment. *Law Enforcement.* Now his short hair and thick-soled shoes made sense. The sudden quiet of an enclosed space made her conscious of how chilled her bare legs were, and her cheeks. And just how loud it had been on the sidewalk, between traffic and people surging by in waves. "Are you a cop?"

"Why, you looking to do something illegal?" One side of his mouth curled up, not quite a smile. "Retired."

"You're young." The apple was a core, now. She bit it in half, chewed. The small seeds, bitter and poison-skinned. Wasn't there arsenic in them? How could she remember that and not her own name, or where she came from?

Turbulence. Her stomach turned over, and bile crawled up into her throat. Evan laughed.

"Yeah, well, thanks." He twisted the key viciously, and the car rocked, startled, a big engine waking inside its mounts. He dropped the Chevy into gear and pavement moved away smoothly under the wheels, bearing Cara along as she chewed the seeds and wondered what she should do with the apple's short, wormlike stem.

In the end, she chewed until it was a frayed, fibrous wad, and swallowed it whole.

4

———

Their destination was a tall concrete block, cookie-cutter windows in neat rows marching along its block-long face. Evan pressed a red intercom button next to a wrought-iron gate with razor wire festooning its ancient bones. A boxy security camera, pointed at the gate's paved bib, held a small red blinking light, and Cara stood out of its likely range. Maybe it was a fake? Evan kept his head down and muttered something she was sure was an obscenity, trapping another cough in that folded red bandanna. Pressed the button again with a blunt, nicotine-stained fingertip.

Cars beetled down each side of the street behind them, waiting patiently for their owners. There were no trees here, just a slim ribbon of cracked sidewalk, the parked vehicles, and a narrow strip of unlined road.

The intercom crackled. "Yes?" A sexless, rasping word.

Evan pressed the button again. "Black hair, blue eyes, short red skirt, long..." He paused, and his eyebrows went up again, amused for some reason. "...brown jacket."

"Between six and six-fifteen?" Static turned every consonant sandpaper-sharp.

Evan glanced at her. "Yeah."

"You're late." Faceless authority hovered behind the camera, and Cara was glad she was outside its field of vision.

Then again, would a nameless woman even be visible to electronic eyes?

"I stopped to take a piss. Sue me." Evan coughed into the bandanna again.

A short humming silence. "You didn't touch the merchandise, did you?"

"Not a finger, Mama. Don't be insulting."

There was another, deeper buzz, and the iron gate clicked open. Evan glanced at Cara. "Come on."

"Merchandise?" Cara glanced over her shoulder, nervously.

"You want to walk away, I won't chase you." He pushed at the gate, gingerly, avoiding the razor wire. "I might even recommend it. She's a bitch."

The intercom fuzzed-chirped again. "I can hear you," the voice said. "Come up, and don't be foolish."

Evan shouldered through the gate. Cara peered after him.

Inside, a small courtyard paved with interlocking stones glowed with green. How on earth did a garden get any sun with the concrete rising on all sides? Blank windows marched along in rising rows, full of shadows since dusk had slid into every crack and corner. None of them were lit; maybe nobody was home from work yet. Leaves rustled and slid, and Cara realized there were no naked branches. Was it all evergreens? A shade garden?

The itching under her skin returned. She hesitated on the doorstep, and Evan's dark hair melded with the dimness. He became part of the undergrowth, shouldering aside long weeping birch-fingers. A breath of clean air filtered onto the smog-choked street, and her lungs filled. Funny, she hadn't noticed the metallic breath of engines burning before now.

Of course she followed. There was nowhere else to go. As soon as she stepped over the threshold it was warmer, the cold wind, knife-cut, falling off. A blank metal door opened, a long wood-walled hallway stuffed with shadows and a faint smell of burning swallowed them both. At the end was a cage of steel, brass, woodwork, and faded red carpet, a semicircle overhead with blank marks.

The antique elevator shuddered, wheezing theatrically as it lifted its cargo. Evan stood slightly in front of her, sometimes glancing back—odd, sipping looks, dark eyes unfathomable. When the contraption shuddered to a stop, warm electric light bathed its open structure. He heaved aside both rattling, groaning doors and stepped out, scanning the hallway before beckoning her forward. A mezzanine stretched in either direction, the central well of the building full of yet more ink-rustling shadows. Old wood glowed and a parquet floor unreeled. Heavy paneling was broken by doors with brass handles, their brass number plates bearing only rubbed-over scratches. Frosted glass sconces held soft-glowing lights, and even inside, the air was fresher. Richer, somehow.

Evan set off, and Cara once again followed. As long as she kept moving in the right direction, the itching, nasty buzz under her skin abated. Her legs ached a little, but not badly. That was strange—spending this long in heels should have turned her lower back into a mess.

Was that something she remembered, or only logic?

The plane. A burst of wine-red terror filled her head, and she stopped, staring blindly. *The plane, what was the flight number?*

"Here we are. Mama Lodi's House." Evan knocked twice

at a door like all the rest. Except its number plate wasn't scratched out, and Cara, her head cocked, stared at it as he knocked again. Shave-and-a-haircut, maybe a signal, maybe a personal joke.

"277," Cara breathed.

"Yep, that's the magic number." Evan frowned, and pitched his voice higher. "Come on, Mama. Open up."

Locks clicked, chunked, and slid aside. The door moved, and more of that golden light spilled out around its borders. Cara's eyelashes fluttered, chopping the image into strobing bits, light and dark revolving before the final impact.

Flight 277 is now boarding...Ladies and gentlemen, we're about to have some turbulence...

"Finally," that gravelly voice said, stripped of electronic edges but still harsh. An old woman in a violently floral housedress and large dark knitted slippers with white fur lining, her nose rising knifelike from a map of parchment skin folded and creased more times than a used napkin, peered through bleached eyes and licked her strong, horse-like yellow teeth. "Come in."

5

———

IT SEEMED IMPOSSIBLE ANYONE COULD BE THIS OLD AND STILL ambulatory. Mama Lodi was bent into a C, and her liver-spotted hands trembled slightly. For all that, she was surprisingly strong, as Cara found out when one of those hands shot out and clamped around her wrist. The woman tugged, and Cara bent. Her face was patted at, and the old woman even examined her mouth, running a papery wrinkled fingertip over Cara's teeth as Evan shut the door. He didn't throw any of the locks.

The urge to bite down, hard, passed through Cara and away. Finally, the old woman huffed out a sigh. "Good enough," she said, and pawed through Cara's pockets, finding nothing, not even lint. She wasn't particularly gentle, either, but the search was impersonal in the extreme.

I could have told you they were empty. Clear, strong instinct warned Cara not to say it, to stare blankly instead of focusing. The nasty, uncomfortable itching had gone away, certainty left in its wake.

"Good enough," the woman repeated, and sucked in a

damp breath. A tang of violets clung to her housedress. "Look at her. A real beauty, huh?"

"Yeah." Evan patted at his own pockets, dropped his hands. "Christ. I could use a cigarette."

"Better if you don't." The old woman laughed, a surprisingly soft, mellifluous sound. Her navy slippers had leathery soles, and they made a faint whispering as she stepped back. "Come in, come in, little girl. Oh, she's very good indeed."

Evan's eyebrows lowered, and he glared at her. "You're forgetting something."

"What would that be?" Her faded gaze, irises muddied but pupils dark wells, lingered on Cara's face. A long, dark hair grew from a mole on the underside of her chin, lustrous and silky. Still, under the ruin of wrinkles, her bones were pretty. You could see a shadow of beauty buried.

Entombed.

"Your end of the deal." Evan folded his arms, legs spread a bit to take up more space. The hallway contained all three of them, and Cara longed to crane her neck, examine her surroundings.

Don't, the instinct warned her, and she listened.

Now the old woman straightened as far as her bent spine would allow and peered up at him, skinny, bony fingers still braceleting Cara's wrist. "You don't want to brace yourself?"

"What the fuck *for*?" He dug in his pocket and brought out the bandanna. Under the warm golden light of the kitchen, dried clots of deeper red caught in its folds twitched as the fabric moved. They dried slowly, pasty-fresh atop crusted ones. "I don't got a lot of time left."

"Are all your affairs in order?" The old woman's colorless tongue touched thin lips. "You can't go back."

"You stalling me?" He crumpled the bandanna in his fist.

His wrists were too large for his forearms. "It's a really bad idea to stall me, Mama."

She shook her head. Her wild mop of thistledown hair, grey shading into white at the roots, barely swayed, caught in a frozen wind. "Not stalling. Just don't want you bitching afterward about unfinished business. Once you do this, you can't go back."

"I'm already dead, for fucksake." Evan's scowl deepened. Stubble roughened his olive cheeks, turned sallow in the warm electric light. "Just do it."

For some reason, that made Mama Lodi laugh. "Come on, then." She shuffled down the hall.

On the left, a living room glowing with beeswax and lemon polish opened up, brass floor lamps with flowering Tiffany stained-glass shades hovering over two thick sofas, a leather armchair with a matching ottoman, a fireplace with an umber glow in its depths. Mahogany shelves held curios —bone, bright feathers, chunks of rock in fantastical quartz-veined colors or deep gemlike glitter. A sideboard-sized, ancient radio crouched between two of the bookcases; a white-painted radiator ticked under an uncurtained window starred with moving lights. Traffic, or stars, wheeled past in steady progression.

Mama Lodi kept going. Past the living room was a doorway opening onto a darkened kitchen with worn blue linoleum and enamel appliances, but she turned hard left and another hallway held one door on the right, one at the end, and an open one on the left showing white pebble-tiles and the clear white glare that said *bathroom*. She pushed the door wide and motioned Evan in, followed him, and beckoned Cara almost as an afterthought.

Four high-intensity bulbs over a sink and a water-clear mirror in a white-pained wooden frame drenched each edge in crisp light. A shell-shaped sink, a tiled countertop, and the two sliding doors of a medicine cabinet sat primly under the mirror. Thick red and white knitted socks vanished into Mama Lodi's slippers and the hem of her housedress. "Strip." Polyester flowers glowed under her skirt, and her bony hands rubbed at each other.

"I hardly know you." Evan's scowl faded.

"You think you've got anything I haven't seen before?"

"What about her?" He tipped his stubbled chin at his shoulder, indicating the younger woman.

"She's a blank wall right now, Detective. Couldn't you tell?"

Did even blank walls observe like Cara did, silently weighing each moment? She stayed at the threshold, her diamanté toes glittering sharply.

"Fine." Evan reached for his tie. Suit jacket, belt, button-down, trousers—he laid his gun in its holster neatly aside, and a golden badge in a black leather case on top of it.

The old woman snatched up the badge; it vanished into a pocket of her voluminous skirt. Next she picked up the trousers, thrusting them at Cara. "Fold those."

So Cara did, slowly, her hands moving all on their own, like they'd done this before. Layers of cloth peeled away, each discarded skin tossed contemptuously at her. The old woman sniffed at Evan's thick-soled shoes and set those next to the gun on the well-scrubbed countertop. Cara folded his boxer briefs neatly and added them to the pile. Bruises marched up and down Evan's ribs, yellow-green ones under fresh redblack ones, and his knuckles were skinned. Muscle had wasted away, and his skin hung a little loosely, used to a much bigger man. He was wasting away.

Cancer, Cara's sure instinct whispered clearly. *In his lungs, and now everywhere else. You can see it.*

If she half-lidded her eyes and let her gaze unfocus, she could. A stain spreading through veins, arteries, internal organs, butterfly wings on an X-ray, shadows wrapping their tentacles through a human body. Quick metastasizing, or he'd let it go too long. A silent killer, bred in breath and blood and bone, fueled by smoke and tar in neat, easy to consume sticks.

The old woman ripped the shower curtain aside and twisted the cold water knob. The bathtub was enameled cast iron, scrubbed and spotless, a pink rubber plug hanging on a chain looped over the old, strong faucet with its two porcelain wagon-wheel eyes, its spout shining. The water sparkled; she dropped the rubber plug over the drain-mouth and chuckled, another surprisingly deep, rich sound. "You know, when you get through this, you'll be able to smoke all you want."

"Can't wait." Evan didn't quite cup his hands over his genitals, but his shoulders hunched like he wanted to. Black hair furred up his chest over much-bruised skin, ran down his flanks. Maybe he'd been stolid before, but the wasting poked his ribs and hipbones out, laying bare angles and bones.

"Oh yes," Mama Lodi crooned into the deepening water. "Stronger, better, faster. That was the deal."

Even Evan's toes held wisps of black fur. His buttocks were nearly flat. "Can we get on with it? This tile's cold."

"If you want to get in before it's finished filling, be my guest." She cackled again when he didn't move. "Better to do it all at once."

"A cold bath is supposed to help me?" Evan half-turned, regarding Cara in the mirror, working the ring off his left middle finger..

The old woman sucked on her strong yellow teeth again,

clicking her tongue for good measure. She watched the water's surface. "You chickening out?"

"No." He glanced at the mirror, again, his coffee-colored gaze meeting hers. "What do *you* think?"

"She won't start thinking for a while." The old woman snort-chuckled. "Not until she has a name."

Evan opened his mouth. Cara held his gaze.

"Huh." He shook his head fractionally, and handed her the ring. "I know a lot of people with names who don't do any damn thinking at all."

Mama Lodi muttered, flicking her fingers in the water. Words dropped from her thin lips, one after another, droplets melding into a single stream of something slow and viscous. Cara's head hurt, a swift piercing pain, and she stepped back, her hip hitting the countertop. Evan's hand moved as if to catch her wrist and she blundered back further, her fist knotting around the lump of metal and its bright blue stone.

"Hurts, does it?" A deep, resonant cackle. "Oh, you brought me a good one for sure." Mama Lodi twisted the water off. Somehow, the tub was almost full, and the fluid's surface ran with a thick opalescent slugtrail sheen. "Come on, Detective. In you go."

6

THE FLUID DIDN'T SPLASH. IT SIMPLY ACCEPTED HIS WEIGHT, moving thickly aside and closing over Evan's wasted legs as he stretched, gingerly. "It's...warm." For a moment, he looked much younger, a boy in a bathtub too big for him.

"Feel silly for bitching?"

"You're an asshole, Mama."

"Takes one to know one." She mumbled again, poking at his hand on the bathtub's rim. "In the water, all of you, or it won't work."

He didn't look at her. Instead, his gaze turned to Cara. "All?"

"Every inch, Detective." Mama Lodi snickered again, peeling his fingers away from the rim. The ring burned in Cara's palm, metal still skin-warm.

Evan's shoulders hunched further. "Does this stuff rinse off?"

"Quit being a baby."

Cara watched as he settled, slipping the ring into her own jacket pocket. His knees dipped below the surface and rose, coated with that thick sheen.

"It's gonna get in my nose."

Mama Lodi, crouched at the tubside, settled back on her thin haunches. "Do you want this, or not?"

"Fine." He shifted again. "I'm gonna have to turn onto my side."

"Then do it."

One shoulder slid below the fluid. Displacement made the slug-sheen rise over him. Tiny fringed fingers of the stuff crawled up, thickening on skin and hair it had already touched. Chewed bits of apple rose in her throat, now seasoned with bile, but she swallowed and her face was safely blank again when Mama Lodi glanced over her shoulder, checking.

Playing dumb was often the safest bet.

"Get everything underneath," the old woman said, softly. "You're almost there, Evan."

"Okay." He took a deep breath, and slid down further.

Mama Lodi's fingers curled over the inky cap of his buzzcut, and she shoved his head under the surface, scooping up more of the thickening stuff and slathering it on the very top of his other shoulder, still bare and innocent. A crackling filled the bathroom, and the old woman laughed. The slug-stuff slopped, and Evan kicked, heels and knees softly thwapping the sides of the tub.

It's holding him down, Cara realized, dreamily.

"Now," Mama Lodi breathed. "Now we make you *perfect*." She raised one dripping hand, using her pointed chin to pull at her shoulder-sleeve a little, like a woman at a soapy sink. Her hand dove again, and Cara took a step forward, exhaling in wonder.

The slug-stuff resisted, but flesh underneath did not. Snakelike, liver-spotted fingers plunged through yielding skin, curled and brought out a chunk of tarlike black bubbling. The old woman hissed balefully, tipping her head at the toilet. Cara understood, and lunged to whisk away Evan's folded clothes, opening the lid. The black stuff went into the bowl with a sickening splash-plop.

Can he breathe? Cara clutched at Evan's clothes. The body under the slug-fluid spasmed again, and the surface of the stuff stretched like plastic wrap.

Another handful of black tar, yanked out and rolled in Mama Lodi's palm like taffy, splashed into the toilet bowl and sank.

"Ohhhh yes." She laughed again. "Perfect, perfect, perfect. Tell me, girl." Another amused, impartial glance. "Are you hungry? You must be *starving*."

"Yes," Cara agreed, even though the nausea threatened to spew half-digested apple all over white tile and enamel.

Plop-splash. "Good. Go out into the kitchen."

Cara blundered out of the bathroom and stood shaking in the hall, still clutching Evan's clothes.

7

———

THE KITCHEN WAS JUST AS CLEAN AND WORN AS EVERY OTHER room. Eggs bubbled in butter, a round black cast-iron skillet on a clean white enamel stove. A coffeemaker sent a thin stream down into its pot, and bacon sizzled.

"He'll be fine." Mama Lodi chuckled, reaching for a sturdy metal spatula. "Now we deal with you, my dear."

That didn't sound welcoming, or even pleasant. "I'm dead," Cara said tonelessly, perched on a plain wooden chair at the small round table. Alive but amnesiac didn't explain the bathtub.

Nothing could explain the bathtub.

"You could be, yes." Mama Lodi nodded. Her long frayed mat of grey and white hair swung. A strap of black leather served her for a belt, cinched tight and gleaming against the violet background of her housedress. "That is an option."

"This is hell?" It was a reasonable guess. Still, she felt alive. Her heart beat, breath filled her lungs, her bare toes tingled when she slid her feet out of the shoes for a few moments, stretching them. She laid her fingertips against her chest. Under the soft black sweater, she *felt* alive.

"Or something else." The old woman tapped the spatula against the side of the egg pan, a soft musical click. "Wheat or white?"

"What?"

"Toast."

A prosaic question, but Cara couldn't even figure out which kind she preferred. Did dead people eat bread? "It doesn't matter."

"Good."

A short while later, a thick white ceramic plate thumped on the red-checked tablecloth in front of her. Wheat toast, scrambled eggs, crispy-melting bacon. The silverware was heavy and glossy, freshly polished. Who cleaned all this—Mama Lodi, her spidery fingers, rubbing with wet rags? Scrubbing the floor bit by bit, on arthritic knees?

"You're probably wondering a great many things." The old woman pulled out the other straight-backed wooden chair and settled a green coffee cup in front of her. "You're lucky. That's the first thing you should know. You've been given a chance to go on living."

"Is this living?" It was a silly question.

"You'll be young and beautiful forever."

Beauty everlasting. A shudder walked cold and liquid down her back, under cashmere and a jacket she couldn't remember but that fit her as if tailored. "If you can do that, how come you're not?"

"I killed my guardian and escaped." Mama Lodi's strong yellow teeth showed, a rictus of merriment. Her hands lay, painfully swollen knuckles red and chapped. "And I waited, getting more and more decrepit, for someone to take my place."

Well, that answered *that.* "Me."

"You."

"What if I don't want to?" Cara touched the fork with a cautious fingertip. A butter-bell stood, upended, next to salt and pepper shakers, a wire holder for paper napkins.

Mama Lodi's left eye blinked, then her right a fraction of a second later. Her fingernails were yellowed too, not from nicotine. The skin and nails were stained in small, intricate patterns, applied so long they had worked through several layers. When you got old, maybe your body simply remembered everything. "Now we give you a name, girl. Pick one you like."

"Cara."

Lodi eyed her suspiciously. "Where did that come from, I wonder?"

She buttoned her mouth and glared at the other woman, ignoring the food. Steam drifted up in thin questing fingers. A cat-shaped clock on the wall swung its long question-mark tail, another heartbeat. Tick-tock, tock-tick.

"Stubborn," Lodi finally said. She leaned back in her chair; it creaked with indignation though she probably didn't weigh enough to be a burden. "Well, too late to back out now. Especially for *him*. Eat."

Cara lifted a piece of bacon, nibbled on one end. Salt stung her mouth, a delicious burn. Hunger woke, a yawning hole inside her guts, and she stuffed the rest of the slice in, chewed, and picked up the heavy, shining fork.

"Good, good." Lodi sucked at her strong yellow teeth. Wiry white hairs stood up on the backs of her wasted forearms, and the mole under her chin quivered a bit. "Appetite's a good sign. Tomorrow, you start work."

"Work?"

"What did you think, you get to sit here in your tower and watch the world go by?" Lodi shook her head. Hr bent spine pointed her sharp chin at the table. "No, little girl."

The eggs were good, fluffy and warm. Toast, dripping with butter, crunched satisfyingly. Cara almost moaned, it felt so good to eat. "What's the work?"

"There are some rules. Only for the first job."

"Why only for—"

"Stop. Asking. Stupid. Questions." Silverware rattled, the window over the sink flushed briefly with red neon, and the metal of the range gave a short, sharp grown, metal cooling too quickly. "Or I'll strangle you."

Cara pushed her feet back into her shoes and loaded a piece of toast with scrambled egg, not looking at the woman. "You'll have to wait for another replacement to come along, then."

"I hate the smartass ones," Lodi muttered. "I've waited this long, I can wait some more."

So there had been others? "Fine." She kept eating.

After a long pause, the old woman lifted her jadeware cup. "Don't touch the bathtub. You interrupt the process now and the good detective could die of shock. Got to let him get out on his own, like a butterfly. Shake those wings and dry them."

"Is he dead too?" Almost-dead? Undead?

"Him? No, little girl, he just traded himself in." Lodi laughed, that impossibly pretty sound brushing painted surfaces, the stove's white enamel, the cabinets. "For a newer model. Heh. You'll understand in time."

8

———

THE BEDROOM WAS SPARE AND WHITE, A NARROW COT WITH tight, bleached linen and a single window that stared over the courtyard garden. Lodi shuffled in, peeked through the glass, and snorted. "Too late to back out," she muttered again, and beckoned Cara. "Come on, look."

Silvery light ran over juicy-fat branches, glowed on stone walkways in a geometric pattern. Vines shifted, crawling over each other, vegetation full of slithering movement. Cara looked up—the sky was faint orange, light pollution bouncing off low clouds. "There's no moon."

"So you *do* have half a brain." Lodi nodded, sucked on her teeth for a moment. "I wondered." A snorting laugh, and she moved away. Cara rested her fingertips on the white-painted sill. Antique window glass, full of bumps and tiny bubbles, solidity caught in ripples as if it remembered being liquid. The dresser was antique too, all its paint scrubbed off. The floor, lightly varnished, reflected white glare from a single bare bulb overhead. "The good detective will sleep here when you return. For tonight, just lie down and think of whatever you want." With another cackle, Lodi jabbed at the switch next to the door.

The bulb died, leaving Cara in a square of soft silvery glow from the window. The door swept shut, and Lodi's steps dragged down the hall. Had she locked it?

Ridiculous. Where was there to go? The snaking garden full of strangeness, or the cold street outside? Finding a police station. *I've lost my memory.*

A warm lump of food in her belly, her calves a little stiff from walking, her lungs filling and deflating regularly. Cara held out her hands, cupping innocent, unnatural moonlight.

The cot-linens smelled of fresh air, of sunlight. Cara tried stretching out in her sweater and skirt, her feet finally able to breathe, and only lasted a few minutes before surging up again. Bare feet on cold wood, she stripped and looked down at her body. Flesh glowed like the window-glass, a lamp in the dark. Breasts, hips, dark pubic fleece —it looked familiar. It *felt* familiar, right down to the white, well-healed scar on her knee.

An identifying mark.

She stretched out again, under two thin blankets and the fragrant sheet. There was a long time of staring at the window trying to remember anything before the silver snake of the baggage carousel. Finally, she fell, soundless as a dry leaf, into the terrifying black abyss of sleep.

9

———————

Garlic. Cooking meat. And...coffee? Good smells tiptoed into the white room, filtered into dreaming, and drew her softly out of a black well. Cloudy grey sunshine spilled through the window's old, rippling glass, and Cara pushed stiff fingers through her hair. Her clothes were right where she left them: skirt, sweater, jacket, shoes. Nothing else, unless she counted the secret cargo of round metal in her jacket pocket.

She carried her shoes down the hall. The bathroom door was half-closed, the light inside making a strange shape on hardwood floor. The urge to peek warred with a strange uneasiness, and she paused on bare feet, considering the door.

"You can look," Lodi called from the kitchen. "But don't touch."

The door creaked, its hinges singing subtle protest. Cara blinked against the brightness multiplied by mirror and white tile, and thin acid touched the back of her throat again.

Scarves and strands of decaying slug-sheen dripped over

the tub-lip, threaded with traces of that tarlike, bubbling black cancer. Lodi hadn't managed to draw it all out of him, perhaps, so the slug-stuff had scrubbed the rest. Or traces of it had ribboned off her liver-spotted hands as she dredged the sickening clumps free.

The commode was clean, white, and innocent. Cara glanced at it, and wondered why she felt no pressure in her bladder. Her mouth held no ghost of last night's bacon, either. She simply felt...awake. And slightly unwashed, but getting into that tub with the slug-stuff melting and gurgling down the drain—no. That made the revulsion at the back of her throat even thicker.

Cutlery rattled. "Don't touch it!" Lodi shrilled, though Cara felt no urge to. "Come out, little girl."

Cara backed out of the bathroom, watching the slug-stuff. A long skein of it stretched, then retracted with a wet sliding sound, and the tub-drain gave a slow bubbling glorp.

She fled down the hall, coming to a heel-bruising halt just inside the kitchen's warm, antique bubble.

The man at the table was...different. The face Evan's, but slightly younger, and his shoulders were broader. The bruises on his arms, bared by a pale cotton T-shirt, were gone. Ropy muscle moved under fine, hairless, newborn skin, and his hair was platinum instead of black now. Even his irises were altered, grey instead of blue.

Bleached.

Photo negative, she thought, and her lips moved soundlessly. Her shoes dangled from one hand; her other hand, wrapped around the side of the doorway, flexed, trying to drive her fingernails into wood, paint, plaster.

Lodi, at the stove, banged the metal spatula. "Don't just *stand* there. Get me some coffee. You're not hungry, he'll eat for you now."

Then why bother with coffee? She opened her mouth to ask, thought better of it, and studied the detective again. A small mountain of steak strips, medium-rare, crouched on his white plate like the world's thickest spaghetti, and a tower of whole-wheat rolls rose on a smaller side-plate. A glass jug of milk sat primly next to a thick jelly-jar glass he filled, then drained in several long swallows. His grey gaze rose and settled on her, not lingering on breasts or hips. Instead, the weight pressed against her face. Did he recognize her?

"There now." Lodi banged the spatula again, picked up the cast-iron skillet, and tumbled several browned sausages onto yet another plate. "Oh, you like that, don't you? Dumb beasts, all of them. Rutting and eating, that's all a man's good for."

Cara stood on one foot to slide her left shoe on, balanced in black patent leather and diamanté buckles to put the right on too. Relief pushed her shoulders back and her chin up—it was probably how knights felt, encased in uncomfortable but comforting armor.

The coffeemaker was a huge silver contraption full of knobs, dials, wands, and a self-contained grinder. Cara ran a fingertip along its top edge, pulling back as a double-scorch —temperature and knowledge—jolted up her arm. *First that button, then that one…you pour the water in there. I see.*

"Things talk to you," Lodi said, slamming the sausage-plate down on the table in front of the detective, who kept chewing. How on earth was he going to fit all that inside him? Was he going to swell up until he burst, a bloodfat tick?

Ticks. She remembered, hazily, walking in sunlit woods, a breeze whispering through summerthick leaves overhead, a meadow full of long grass and small blue flowers. As soon as it appeared the image faded, and she found her hands moving, tamping down ground coffee and twisting the holder into its socket, flicking a switch and sliding a small white ceramic cup under a pair of metal teats. Espresso streamed out, brown froth lining each edge of the liquid stream, and the heavenly, lying scent of fresh coffee drifted against the heaviness of browned meat.

"Bring that here. You're a slow one, aren't you. Well, I suppose I wasn't much different at the beginning." Lodi made a spitting sound, her thin lips pursing, and jostled the back of the man's chair with her hip. "Eat, don't stare at her. You'll have all the time you want to look later. Might even get sick of it."

The old woman snatched the ceramic cup from Cara's fingers, tossed the contents back all in one gulp. "Even that tastes like sand," she continued. "Came along just in time, you two did. Go make yourself some, now, and we'll get started."

"Get started on what?" Cara backed away as the old woman glanced at her. She decided it wasn't an unreasonable or stupid question and halted, folding her arms.

"Getting fresh, aren't you." Lodi cackled. "It's a nice change. I'll tell you everything you need to know, little girl. So make yourself some coffee, and let's begin."

Lodi folded her veiny, age-spotted hands. "It's simple. He'll take you to a place. You'll have a nice dinner with a nice family. Afterwards, the father will give you a package, which you will take to a certain building, knock on a certain door, and deliver it to a man who paid for the service. Then you come home."

It did sound simple. Cara held her own tiny ceramic cup

of fragrant, steaming liquid and glanced at Evan. He kept eating, mechanically, strip after strip of steak vanishing into his mouth. Chewing slowly but thoroughly, swallowing like clockwork. His gaze settled on her face again, and he nodded slightly as if she'd spoken.

"Now, the rules. Once you step outside for this first job, you speak only to him until you get back in the door here. If you have a question, you ask *him*. They can hear and answer, but that doesn't concern you. Directly address anyone else and it's all over."

"What happens?"

"You take my age, and I'm free as a bird with yours."

"Can he talk?"

"Of course he can."

Cara looked at Evan. "Are you sure?"

He swallowed, coughed to clear his throat. His voice, husky, had grown deeper. "Yes, I can."

Well, that was good. "How do you feel?"

Lodi snorted. The window over the sink was full of golden light, richer than the overhead fixture's illumination. The one in the bedroom was full of rainy winter, instead.

Cara's head hurt again, a sharp piercing spike. She exhaled, softly, and kept her gaze on Evan's.

"Better," he said, a spark struggling in his grey eyes. "Stronger."

"Did it hurt?" Cara lifted the cup, wished she hadn't because his gaze focused on her mouth.

"A little." A slight shrugging motion of those broad shoulders. Under the table, he wore jeans and engineer boots with thick, rubbery soles. Muscle moved in his forearms, denuded of their black forest. A male presence, taking up all available space, squeezing Lodi and Cara into the margins.

Except when he looked at her, she expanded, too. A strange feeling, her jacket pocket far too heavy for the small lump of metal it carried. "Was it what you wanted?"

Lodi snorted. "Who the hell knows what they want?" she asked her own coffee, her proud high nose wrinkling. The gold light drained some essential solidity from her papery skin and matted hair, a dusty antique doll with beady, wicked eyes on a high shelf.

"I didn't ask *you*," Cara snapped. The woman was irritating. Vexation was a tonic, running down her arms and legs, much better than any caffeine kick.

The old woman subsided with a malevolent grumble.

Evan took a long drink of milk, and when he finished, he looked much more awake. Less of a somnolent eating machine. "I don't know," he said, finally. "I was dead anyway."

All that cancer, riddling his body—well, he probably wasn't far wrong. Cara took another sip, and shifted a little to face Lodi. "What happens to you once we finish this?"

"I get to move on." The old woman's face screwed up, an apple-granny puckermask. A tiny, queer gleam filled her tired, worn eyes, and she lingered over the words one by one, a private joke. "Staying between is boring as fuck after a few hundred years. People are stupid, especially the ones you look at every day."

Well, she certainly looked old. It made as much sense as anything else did, here. "What's in the package? The one we're picking up?"

"Don't ask. It doesn't matter." Lodi rested her elbows on the table. Her grin turned predatory, lazy, the satisfied thin-lipped look of a cat who is quite full but still watches a small struggling thing. "Just do this one simple thing, and it'll all be settled."

"It's never just one simple thing." Evan returned to his slow, steady consumption, ignoring the glare Lodi darted in his direction.

Cara sipped espresso. Bitterness balanced with rich aroma, and it vanished somewhere behind her breastbone. No hunger, no thirst. Yes, they were both dead anyway. "The espresso machine wasn't there yesterday."

Lodi cackled softly. "The place'll change for you, over time. One of the perks."

If this was heaven, it was annoying. If it was hell, it wasn't terrifying enough. Purgatory, perhaps. "Good to know."

"Self-cleaning." Lodi waggled her eyebrows, poisonous caterpillars clinging to a gnarled forehead-branch.

"The housewife's friend," Cara finished. Who needed a name when you could remember advertising jingles?

"Oh, we're far more than pearls and oven cleaner, little girl." Lodi smacked her withered palm on the table, and cutlery danced. "Go get ready. When he finishes breakfast, you're out the door."

PART II

MUNDI ÆTERNA

10

———

THE COURTYARD GARDEN, ENCLOSED IN FOUR SLABS OF HIGH, window-pierced concrete, glowed under directionless sunlight. It should have been deep in artificial gloom, since clouds thickened over the visible square of sky overhead. Yet gold edged every branch and vine, and when Cara's fingers brushed against a low, olive-leafed shrub she stopped.

Boil the sap down, and it's poison. Dry the leaves, aromatic. Weave the branches in a wreath before they turn dry-brittle, and catch passing gazes...

Her ankle turned and she almost staggered, her skirt swaying. Sun-heat brushed her bare knees, and Evan's hand closed around her elbow. "You okay?" A sleek, hip-length leather jacket, shrugged over the white T-shirt, covered up his shoulder-holster and the gun. He'd had to loosen the straps a bit, because he was...bigger.

No wonder he'd needed to eat.

"Fun, isn't it?" Lodi grinned, her violently floral house-coat swinging. "Gloves won't help. You'll know, no matter what, so be careful what you touch. Now, you know where to go?"

Evan nodded. "It's in here." He tapped at his temple with his free hand. "Everything is."

"Now remember, don't talk to anyone but him." Lodi swayed from foot to slippered foot, as if the paved path pained her. "He knows what to do and where to go."

Cara touched a slim sapling with paper-white bark. *Birch. Betula pendula. The keys will open doors.* Was it just her hands, or her entire skin? She could test it, but not with Lodi all but spitting with impatience and making shooing motions. Evan, his hand still cupping her elbow, drew her along. "It's all right," he said, softly. "I'll take care of you."

"Mine said that to me, too." Lodi snarled. "Go, and come back so I can finish up. I've earned it." That same cat-sharp grin lingered around her thin lips, folded her eyes up in wrinkled fleshy pouches.

Cara pushed her heels down, tipping her head back to look at Evan. Those bleached eyes, fringed with platinum lashes, quiet but not quite blank, not anymore. His jawline was the same, and his cheekbones. The slug-stuff had merely leached the color from him, and rebuilt him a little larger.

And pulled that tarlike blackness from his lungs, his bones, his liver. Whatever else he'd lost in the transaction, that had to be a good thing.

"All right," she said. "I trust you."

"Sickening." Lodi's voice was the angry, reedy whine of a cricket. "Get *going*."

"Shut up," Cara replied, and freed her elbow with a decided motion. Evan set off down the path and she followed, restraining the urge to touch the gate, the wall, another branch, to feel that soundless jolt of information poured into her skull wholesale.

He paused at the gate, looking over his shoulder. She

hurried to catch up, and the gate-hinges groaned. It swung wide, and as she stepped through, winter chill replaced sun-warmth.

Cara shivered.

His car was parked in the same spot half a block from the gate, though a pall of dusty road-grime now covered it and scattered leaves had gathered under its tires. The parking permit was gone and the windshield was dappled with several layers of raindrops and dust. The license plate on the front bumper, caked with mud, rippled strangely when she peered at it, sending another quick needle-pain through her skull.

Evan closed her in on the passenger side. The engine roused swiftly when he turned the key—apparently it hadn't been standing long enough to drain the battery. Or was that more magic?

Of course, that was the only word that applied.

The car shook, the engine seating itself more firmly. *Turbulence*, Cara thought, and a shudder raced through her from crown to soles. Cold air soughed through the car's vents, and her hands knotted against each other, clutching so tight small bones creaked.

It pulled away from the kerb, a small ship on smooth seas, and Evan's hands settled on the wheel. Creeping along just over the speed limit, whooshing within a few feet of other parked cars, anonymous shapes standing in patient rows. How many of them were waiting for people to come back? Who *lived* around here, anyway? Was Lodi's building full of other amnesiacs?

She could ask, at least. "Are there others? In Lodi's building?"

"Never seen any." He glanced at her, returned his attention to the road. His hair glowed. "Or heard 'em, either. Don't think she's the neighborly type."

"No, I suppose not." It felt good to speak, she decided. Especially without the old woman snapping at every sentence. The seat was plush instead of vinyl, so bare skin wouldn't stick. "Are you really okay?"

"Best I've felt in years." He stretched his fingers, one at a time, each with a tiny half-moon of fresh white nail. His wrists were no longer too large. "Cara, right?"

"Yeah." She'd picked the name. Maybe she could pick another. A terrifying thought, taking off names like coats, trying them on, deciding—but how could you ever be sure who you truly were after you had a few? If you married you had a new name, you could file paperwork and change it—hadn't there been an artist who changed his to a symbol?

Names were magical, too.

"I wasn't supposed to bring you the apple." His tone dropped, a dry-throat confession. "I was supposed to eat it when I picked you up."

"I was hungry." A lie. Would she ever feel hungry again? *He'll eat for both of you.*

"I could tell. You even ate the core."

The engine warmed up, the air blowing through the vents too. Could she touch the dash, tell if the car had a previous owner? It didn't smell like stale smoke and aftershave anymore, simply of cold and disuse. "Do you...what do you remember?"

"Uh, everything. Except the bathtub, I guess. Whatever that stuff was. You?"

"Nothing." Tighter, and tighter.

Evan reached over. His fingers were warm, and his hand covered both of hers. "Don't worry." Kindly. "You're all right now. Once we're done with this, we can find out who you are."

"You promise?"

"Sure. I was a detective, remember?" He squeezed, gently. It almost hurt; she flinched, and Evan snatched his hand away. "Sorry. It, uh. That stuff did something. I broke two plates this morning just picking them up."

Dried leaves scattered across the road, swept by the stiff bristles of a cold wind. He took a left, then a right, then a thoroughfare opened up on either side.

"It made you stronger," Cara finally said. "It took the cancer out, too." A thin cold trickle went through her. *Magic* was definitely the word that applied. And he was carrying a gun, too.

It was too late to make any sort of protest. An amnesiac straw on a current, borne along.

"Yeah. I'll be careful." He paused, and the car nosed into the creeping traffic. Horns blared; unruffled, he nudged into the far lane. "What do you remember?"

*A grimace, lips stretched too far, crimson rubbed between the teeth, the blonde woman's head flopping loosely on a snapped neck...*Cara shook the mental image away. "I don't know." It was finally warm enough, and she stopped shivering. Would she wear this skirt, this sweater, for the rest of her existence? Money was necessary. Where did Lodi's food come from?

Shopping. Driving. The daily minutiae of a life. How could she remember that, but not her own name?

"It's going to take a while." A bar of sunlight fell across Evan's profile, turned his bleached hair into a nuclear winter.

Yes, Cara decided. It would. But apparently, she had time now.

11

———

A MASSIVE BRICK HOUSE SQUATTED ON A HILL, A BLACK RIVER of a freshly sealed driveway rising and curving back. The bleached bones of a dry fountain rose in the middle of the drive's arc, and ropes of twinkling blue and white lights were wrapped around columns, skeletal leafless bushes, the roofline, outlining all the windows. A crystal-clear bay window held a sword of stars and tinsel, slow-dying wood hung with color-coded decorations.

Evan's car had somehow acquired a glossy coating, sleek and lower lines. Cara rubbed at her eyes once, decided it was useless, and closed them. The engine cut off, and he exhaled, sharply.

"Remember the rules," he said. "Okay?"

It took two tries to clear her throat. "Okay." *I didn't ask what happened to him if I don't.* Probably nothing nice.

"Wait," she said, as he reached for the door handle. "Here." She dug in her jacket pocket, and dropped the rung into his palm.

"Oh, man." Evan eyed its glitter, touched the blue stone with a large blunt fingertip. "What happened to my badge?"

"Lodi took it."

"Figures." His fingers closed, wrist swelling as he made a fist. He exhaled, hard, and she wondered if she'd made a mistake. "Thank you. It...man, I wouldn't like to lose this. It was my dad's."

He had a father. A past. Cara looked down at her own naked, ahistorical hands as he tested the golden circle on one finger, then another. It fit on his left hand, third finger.

Like a wedding ring. "Cara? I mean it. Thank you."

"You're welcome," she said, numbly, and waited for him to open his door.

Westering sunlight, winter-thin, broke briefly over the house's brick façade before vanishing behind a scrim of icy clouds. The A low cold wind rattle-mouthed the bushes, their naked arms full of white lop-prune scars. A wreath on the huge, red-painted double doors glowed green and silver, both colors plastic-vivid. Its ribbons waved stiffly as Cara followed Evan's wide black-coated shoulders, his hair glowing above the collar.

He didn't ring the doorbell. Instead, he rapped his knuckles on thin hollowcore wood. *Thack-thack.* A pause. *Thack.*

The door shuddered, and Cara had a vivid image of him drawing back one fist, punching, and the entire front of the house falling down, dust and bricks and—

He glanced back at her, and she had the uncomfortable feeling he shared the thought. A radio tuned to her broadcast. His arm tensed, but she hurriedly looked away at the dry fountain and the ruthlessly clipped bushes.

The door swung inward. A broad-hipped black-haired woman with a round brown face peered from atop a white-and-buff uniform. Her ankles bulged a bit over scuffed, thick-soled white shoes, and she shook her head once, heavy, beautiful hair swaying in a tight scraped-back pony-tail. "Come in," she whispered, hunching her large, soft shoulders. "Take your jacket sir?"

The uniform, shiny rigid cloth, looked uncomfortable, and her shoes squeaked a bit as she stepped aside. Evan shook his head as her soft plump hands fluttered, Cara smiled as hard as she could, likewise refusing the woman's ministrations. Small gold hoops glittered in the woman's ears, and Cara opened her mouth to say *no thank you* like a mannerly child...

...and caught herself. Did she really believe Lodi? *You take my age, I take yours.*

On the other hand, there was the slug-stuff in the bath-tub, heaving itself down the drain with soft slippery sounds. And the almost-white feathering of stubble along Evan's nape, hair ruthlessly trimmed and leached.

Magic. So she closed her lips, and simply followed Evan down the hall. The woman at the door made some sort of faint protest, and Cara longed to say something polite, something kind.

The floor was laminate, each step clicking under her heels. The entryway was high and drafty, stairs curving up on either side. A chandelier tinkled softly overhead, hard sharp glitters and two tiny burned-out bulbs like missing teeth. Music played softly, a watered-down version of three kings rollicking towards a hanging star.

"Who is it?" A soft female voice echoed overhead. Scur-rying footsteps, and a lacquer-haired, bone-thin woman appeared at the balustrade. "Oh. John, it's for you. *John!*" A slight, frantic edge to the name—of course, her nose lifted a little, and everything from her taupe pantsuit to her expensive fingernails said that she would have preferred them to wait on the step while someone carried their name upstairs for a decision on admittance. "He's in his office."

"Thank you." Evan's voice boomed in the high-arched space, and Cara almost jumped. Warm air touched her cheeks, her bare calves, stirred her hair. "We'll wait in the den."

The woman's thick-plastered face crinkled for a moment, and her russet hair held the same too-intense tint as the door-wreath. It didn't move as she leaned forward a little. Too urbane to gawk, instead she peered over the balustrade, and her nude lipstick cracked at the edges of her mouth. Her earrings were gold, too, but not as mellow-beautiful as the other woman's. They clicked, a cascade of tiny trash-metal bones, and Cara pushed her hands into her jacket pockets.

She didn't want to know what they might tell her.

The den was vinyl masquerading as leather, a bookshelf with color-coded titles, and a massive flatscreen television, muted but glowing, its huge face beaming a news report over couches and a polar-bear skin that was, thankfully, not real. Its fur, rough acrylic, shone in a drench of electric light from heavy brass-colored fixtures, and a fireplace with a gas insert ran with orange flame.

On the screen, a blonde woman's eyebrows lifted slightly as her mouth moved. The inset on the left half of the screen showed a broken aluminum skeleton reclining against the side of a mountain whose top had been scraped flat in the quest for coal. A pall of smoke hung over its bed. Young stunted pines ringed the site, some scorched and flattened from the impact. *FLIGHT 277*, the chyron said, breathlessly. *NO SURVIVORS FOUND.*

Cara's hands knotted, slick-palmed, inside her pockets. Evan stalked across the room, his right boot passing within an inch of the bearskin's black plastic nose, and scooped up a king-sized remote. It took two tries, jabbing it at the screen, before the wreckage faded, its ghost scorched onto her retinas.

"Shoulda put my fist through it. You want a drink?" Evan turned on his heel, stalking for a sideboard that was supposed to look like walnut. A strange chemical sweetness filled the entire room—air freshener. Still, a thread of fir— oily, rasping, *real*—floated to her as well. The tree was upstairs, balanced on a strip over the entryway, peering through the window, and of course there would be no room underneath it for presents. Only empty, glittering boxes. "I want a drink."

"Yes," she heard herself say, numbly. *God, do I ever.*

She suspected, however, it would have no effect.

12

John was tanned, fit, and in an expensive, lightly starched Egyptian-cotton shirt, sleeves rolled up to show waxed forearms. He entered the den with heavy confidence and a bright white smile, his loafers polished and tied neatly, and stopped for a moment, perplexity wrinkling his brow for a bare moment. "Oh. Hi. They didn't say there'd be two of you."

"Is that a problem?" Evan grinned, his teeth just as white. He handed Cara a small glass carrying an inch and a half of brown alcohol. "His whiskey's good, at least," he murmured.

She took the drink and tossed it far back. It might as well have been water.

"Not a problem at all." John strode forward, hand out. "Just remarking. John. John—"

"You sure you want me to know?" Evan extended his own hand and met John halfway. "I'm Smith. This is the missus."

We're married now? A horrible, pointless desire to laugh

pooled in Cara's throat with the remains of the phantom liquor. A faint warmth began behind her breastbone.

"Well, Officer Smith—"

"Detective," Evan said.

John's jaw set. It was, Cara had to admit, satisfying to watch. Even more satisfying was John's wince when Evan squeezed—probably gently, or he would have ground broken phalanges together.

"*Detective* Smith," John said, "I hope you won't mind staying for dinner? We're having pork roast tonight, it's Conchita's specialty." Movement thumped and thudded overhead. Cara's mouth dried out. Children? It seemed unimaginable, little humans here. "That's John Junior. Do you like children, Mrs Smith?"

I don't know. Cara ducked her head a little, letting her hair veil her expression. It was easy to step behind Evan and watch the assumptions slide over John's face—a little grudging, his gaze settling briefly on her chest before skittering guiltily back to her presumed owner.

"She loves 'em." Evan knocked back his own drink. "You have a son?"

"Spitting image. I'll bet May is telling Conchita to set another couple places. Come on, we'll open a bottle of wine."

It was easy to let them talk, to drift after Evan, her steps making crisp little sounds against paper-thin laminate. She almost preferred Lodi's apartment—well, not almost, she *did* prefer it. At least the things there were...solid.

Conchita was the woman who had opened the door. Faint dark rosettes bloomed on shiny fabric under her arms, and she darted a bleak glance at the men as the dining room opened up around Cara—a long table with a thick cotton tablecloth, a large earthenware pot on a heavy trivet taking pride of place. The centerpiece, pushed aside, was dying sunflowers in a strange bone-colored bowl, their stems held in place by a crushing load of glass pebbles. Five places were laid, and the very thin woman in taupe was already there, fussing over folded napkins not quite thick enough to be real linen.

John Junior was a heavy-shouldered, round-faced young man in a crumpled basketball uniform under a red hoodie. The uniform, royal blue and violent yellow polyester, made him a bright blot against the beige walls and long swathes of glass overlooking a ruthlessly clean, winterized concrete patio. A shrouded patio table overlooked a forlorn strip of marshy lawn before a high board fence broke the view. "You didn't say anything about guests," he whisper-hissed at the thin woman, whose lipsticked mouth set bitterly.

"Be *polite*," she whispered back, and he pulled out his chair, its high cushioned back driving into her hip. She grimaced and hurried towards the kitchen, separated from the dining room by a low island topped with heavy false marble.

"It smells good!" John rubbed his hands together, then lifted the lid on the massive earthenware pot. A ceramic trivet underneath all but groaned at the weight. "Junior, you're gonna apologize to your mother when she comes back. There, and there." He indicated two seats, and Evan pulled a chair out, waiting for Cara to settle in it. When she did, he leaned over her slightly, pushing it in, and a hot flush worked up her cheeks.

"Thank you," she murmured, and wished she hadn't, because John's gaze settled on her again, cold as leftover coffee.

"Shy, is she?" A hearty, hollow laugh. "I remember when May was like that."

"What?" The thin woman turned away from her fierce, huddled conference with Conchita, whose head had pulled turtle-like between her shoulders. "Are you lying about me again?"

"Just saying I remembered when we were first dating." John glanced at his son. "Sit up, please. Don't slouch."

"There won't be enough left," the child sulked. "Did Conchita make rice?"

"I'm sure she did. She knows how much you like it."

May returned, sunflower-patterned oven mitts cradling a wide, steaming wooden bowl. "Rice. There's the salad—John, will you..." The words died on her thin lips. "I'll get it, never mind."

Evan touched Cara's shoulder. "Don't," he said, since she had tensed to rise again. "I'll get it, sweetheart."

Which left her at the table with John and John Junior, both of them staring. The boy fiddled with the stamped metal cutlery, and finally smiled. "She looks weird."

"Junior." His father's hand landed on his wrist, and the boy winced. Dull brick-red crept up his cheeks. "Apologize."

"Sorry," he muttered.

Cara reached for her wineglass. It was empty.

John leapt to his feet to pour, his thighs hitting the edge of the table with a dangerous *thunk*. The centerpiece rattled. "He's just not used to beautiful women."

For the second time, Cara almost said something. *What about your wife?* The words trembled on the tip of her tongue, but instead, she glanced at Evan's broad back. He hadn't taken his jacket off, either. So she simply shook her head and dropped her gaze, watching as straw-yellow wine trickled into her glass.

It was probably cheap, but she knew she'd drink it anyway.

13

SLICED PORK WITH MUSHROOMS ON A BED OF WILD RICE, salad with a plastic jar of vinaigrette. It could have fed twice their number, but Junior still whined that he didn't get enough. Conchita glided through the dining room, her raven head down and a massive handmade leather purse tucked high up under her arm. Her ponytail longed to burst free of its confinement, her hair impossibly vital. "I go for dessert," she said, softly, and May waved her away with a pained smile and a hand with a glittering engagement ring.

"That's fine, Conchita." After a long moment, she added a grudging thank-you, glancing at Cara.

May ate in slivers—a minuscule fragment of pork, a few grains of rice, and between each mouthful she cut Junior's pork into bite-size pieces for him. John, with pained courtesy, handled his knife and fork Continental-style, and stared at Cara's breasts while he attempted conversation with Evan.

"Most cases are simple," Evan said, after a bite of rice. Gone was the mechanical shoveling of fuel into his mouth; instead, he took only morsels, and glanced at Cara every now and again as if for confirmation. "You just follow the dots."

That perked Junior up. "You mean like murders? You solve murders?" He swung his legs,

His mother made a disapproving noise, but Evan smiled.

"Sometimes." He took a sip of water, set the glass down with a small precise noise. "It's pretty much just people fighting over money."

"It's a jungle out there, huh?" John stabbed at a slice of pork. "Dog eat dog."

The rice was perfectly textured, the mushrooms still retaining some vigor. Still, it was flavorless, maybe because Cara avoided the meat. She pushed her portion around her bone-colored plate, spreading it to look consumed. The wine smelled harsh, almost vinegary, and its bite against her palate was something she remembered. Perhaps that was why she kept drinking, its faint alcoholic warmth simply vanishing behind her breastbone.

"Money or women." Evan's knee bumped Cara's under the table. She moved away, crossing her ankles. Laid her fork down. It was useless, the food wasn't even sawdust. It was simply...empty. Each time her bare skin touched the tablecloth, she had a dim sense of Conchita laying dishes down, her plump hands arranging each item carefully and a bright spear of hate revolving inside her softness. Or loud voices, fists pounding, glacial silences, a child's sobbing. The fork only held a ghost of water and detergent; Cara wished she had gloves. Jeans. Bandages, to wrap herself like a mummy.

Lodi said it wouldn't work, but it was worth a try. Anything was.

"One or the other." John grinned. "Right, May? Every man's downfall."

The thin woman shook her head, her earrings swinging. "You're vulgar, John." Her next forkful was an almost-whole mushroom instead of one cut in half.

"Vulgar. That's her way of saying something's too expensive." The tanned man brayed with laugher, took another bite, chewed thoroughly. A faint sheen glistened on his forehead.

Junior had other questions. His dark hair lay flat and lank, and he scratched at the back of one thick wrist. A small red arc preparing to sprout acne nestled in the crease under his lower lip. "What's the worse murder you saw? I mean, bodies. Were there maggots?"

"Junior! We're *eating*." May's distaste mounted; she forked another mushroom carefully up.

The boy pushed his lower lip out. "You hardly eat anyway." He swung his legs again, vigorously, kicking the table's central support. The centerpiece clattered, sunflower heads swaying.

"Got to keep a girlish figure." John smacked his hand down on his son's wrist again. "*Stop* that."

May set her cutlery down. She folded her hands in her lap and stared at her plate. Her cheeks gleamed, not with a flush but with deadly paleness under a thick pall of foundation.

"Oh, now she's going to sulk. Conchita will bring back dessert, but she won't have any." John grinned even wider. His nostrils flared. "Would you like to be excused, wife?"

She glanced at Cara, venomously. "We have *guests*," she hissed, as if the other woman had somehow insulted her.

I'm sorry. Cara swallowed the words. She could say something to Evan, but what was the point?

"You want a drink, detective?" John rose, bumping the table again. He tossed his cotton napkin onto his ravaged plate. Steam still lifted form the earthenware pot. "I want a drink."

"John..." May's lips were bloodless now too. Her hands turned into fists in her lap, crumpling her own napkin. "*John...*"

Junior slumped against the back of his chair. He coughed, and bits of rice spattered against his plate. He blinked furiously, eyelashes fluttering.

Cara gasped. The spat rice was *red*.

May stiffened in her chair. Her eyes rolled up, only the whites showing as she turned into a single bone, scraped clean and bleached. A sudden bathroom stink roiled under the table and Junior pitched sideways, kicking again as muscle spasms rolled through him. Dishes, silverware, glasses all danced.

"What..." John choked, bending over as if punched. "*Fuuuuuuuuu...*" The word trailed off on a long huff, and when the next cramp seized him he doubled even further, his forehead landing in the middle of his plate with a solid, shattering thud. Blood sprayed, rich crimson, and May's head tipped back, her jaw working, teeth grinding and jaw popping as muscles locked down.

It was the mushrooms. Conchita was long gone.

14

———

THE FRIDGE WAS A TOP-OF-THE-LINE SILVER MONSTER, CAPABLE of dispensing water and ice, its sides and front innocent of any pictures, notes, or memorabilia. Evan dug in its glaring white innards, opening drawers. Bottles clinked, a half-full container of generic soymilk sloshed. "What a relief."

Cara folded her arms across her belly. Her legs trembled, the big muscles in her thighs on the verge of rebellion. The kitchen island's countertop pushed into her hip, holding her steady. "They're dead," she repeated, perhaps stupidly.

Evan's hair glowed in the flood of harsh refrigerator light. "Probably."

"Did you know that would happen?" That terrible sharp bathroom stink of failed sphincters mixed with chemical air freshener. Upstairs, a television muttered and babbled, speaking to itself in an empty room.

"She said after dinner the package would be in the fridge." He found what he was looking for in one of the very bottom drawers. A bag of red and yellow peppers glowed, bottles of vile-green soda too. Packets of pressed lunchmeat and sliced soy cheese stood in neat stacks. Perhaps this was Conchita's territory? The triple sinks, brushed and metallic, were ruthlessly clean as well, except for a single quarter-full water glass. The dishwasher hummed, clearly audible now in the stinging silence.

"The package." Cara glanced over her shoulder, nervously, wished she hadn't. May still sat bolt-upright, her helmet of carefully arranged hair glistening, her hands knotted in her lap and her head thrown back. Her lips were pulled back, exposing well maintained teeth, but tiny crimson threads ran between each ivory nugget. Junior had fallen sideways and sprawled on the laminate floor, his legs tangled with his chair and his father's. John, bent over, his forehead grinding into the broken plate, was a rigid, balanced sculpture. A large wet brown stain blossomed at the seat of his khakis. "What is it?"

"Don't know." He held it up, a fist-sized chunk wrapped in brown paper and tied with string. "Feels squishy. You want to carry it?"

No. She did *not*. "Do I have to?"

"Look for something to put it in, then."

A search in the well-ordered pantry behind a sliding plywood partition came up with a collection of reusable grocery bags, each with a high-end store's name blazoned on the side. Cara chose a burlap one, the least decorated of the bunch, and Evan dropped the wrapped lump into it. The fridge door swung shut with a heavy sound.

"Should we call..." *Call the cops?* That was a normal thing to do in this situation, right? Normal did not apply anymore. Cara swallowed the last half of the sentence and shook her head.

"They might run the housekeeper down." Evan shook

his pale head. "I don't blame her. Probably paying her under the table, and not enough either."

The world greyed out. It came back with a rush, and Cara found her forehead against Evan's chest, a high healthy vital heat spreading from his skin. A tang of leather, the slight musk of a clean male animal, and a faint throbbing sense of his heartbeat surrounded her.

"Shit," he said, softly. "It's okay. It's all okay. Nothing's gonna happen to you."

What a useless thing to say. It had *already* happened. Her heart beat, her breath came in and out, and she'd just eaten poison.

Magic. Bloody, murderous magic. May's head, tilted back, and her crimson-threaded smile reminded Cara of a blonde woman with the same smile, a rattling and jolting, screaming, sky and earth changing places in quick succession.

We're about to experience some turbulence, folks. A man's voice crackling over an intercom, and the animal of fear inside every human stomach turned into a frightened, quivering rabbit.

"It's all right." Evan kept saying the same soothing, the same soothing, nonsensical words. "Nothing will hurt you. I promise."

There was nothing more to fear; the hurt had already happened. Her shaking was not grief or terror, but something else entirely, something Cara—it was as good a name as any—was certain she had never felt before in her other life. Or if she had, she had buried it too far beneath her conscious mind to ever let it surface.

Because massive, white-hot rage was not what a good girl was raised to feel.

15

—————

"We're gonna go to place," Evan said, the car dropping into reverse. It had clouded over, the sky a flat iron pan. "Peachwood. Bad neighborhood." He put his arm over the back of her seat, watching as he steered, and the heat of him was now familiar.

Cara settled the burlap bag between her ankles. The lump inside radiated cold knowledge, pressing against her ankles. At least it was wrapped. The seat was cold, too, plush nosing behind her bare knees.

The car shifted into drive, and he retreated to his own seat as metal, rubber, glass, and passengers slid out of the driveway. "Say something," Evan said.

Where had Conchita gone? Did she have a car?

A pale blot tangled in a leafless sapling, and Cara blinked. It was cheap shiny cloth, dark under the armpits, a seam ripped along the back closure. The zipper's fabric tape hung, a lolling tongue, and Cara saw Conchita stepping out of the hideous, cheap uniform, her undergarments melting into comfortable jeans and a brightly colored sweater, her beautiful raven hair bursting free of its tight ponytail, her earrings shining suns. A smile, a flash of rainbow brilliance and white teeth, and the woman was gone, running lightly as her arms lifted gracefully, and when she lifted free of the earth, Cara's heart lifted too.

Maybe that was what had happened. If magic was real, if Cara was still dead-not-dead, then maybe the other woman was something strange and lovely, too. And flying, free.

Beauty everlasting.

"How did you meet Lodi?" she heard herself ask, and felt the small, internal *click* of a right question, finally. One, perhaps, she should have asked earlier.

Evan glanced at her as the car threaded through the subdivision, winter dusk gathering along cul-de-sacs and greenbelts, streetlamps shimmering into life. Tiny pinpricks of precipitation dotted the windshield. "Everyone knew about crazy old Lodi," he said, finally. "At the precinct."

More bare branches rattled, and the other subdivisions trotted past. Bell Ridge. Hathaway. Summer Glen. Smaller, shabbier homes under lamps of a different color squeezed onto narrow lots. Then they mushroomed, apartment complexes instead of single dwellings, but the names didn't change much. A few lamps didn't kindle, standing dark sentinel in winter dusk.

Finally, Evan spoke again. "The old cops said she could do things, Vice said she had a finger on the pulse."

"What kinds of things?"

"You know. Things." *Magic*, his tone said, bluntly. The ring's stone glowed, a blue eye. "Anyway, she does all sorts of stuff. She'll pass information, that gives you an edge. If you bring her something she wants, she'll help you out. Like that."

"What did you bring her?"

He glanced at her, a flash of pale irises. "You. But it wasn't the first time." The misting turned into sleet, each raindrop with a dot of ice at its heart.

"You brought her other people?"

"No. Just things. Information sometimes. Once or twice a gun, or something…" He paused. "I shouldn't be telling you this."

"It's not like it matters." What was she going to do, report him?

His forehead wrinkled. "You shouldn't have to hear about things like that."

"She wants me to take over, right?" So that was Lodi's business. Magic for cops.

"I guess." He tapped the brakes, turned the wipers on. Headlight glow splashed them both. Day died rapidly at this end of the year, especially when the buildings rose to absorb what little sun made it through cold, heavy clouds. "I always got the feeling she didn't have to, she just…likes it."

More apartment complexes. Forest Mill, though there was no forest and no mill. There were no ridges or glens, either. Just pavement and small dwellings, business zones prying with sharp fingers and "bargain" prices as rent grew more and more precarious. Traffic thickened, people coming home, and a spatter of thin, icy sleet touched the windshield.

He turned right on another street. Lights flashed—a fire truck, two police cars, an ambulance snarling traffic on the other side. Onlookers in heavy coats and hats gathered on the sidewalk, faces slack with awe or trepidation, pressing between parking meters and stoplights. A small storefront was shattered, glass twinkling under headlight splashes. The sleet intensified.

"Looks like a robbery." Evan's right hand twitched, probably itching for a nonexistent radio. "Shit."

The engine had warmed again; Cara no longer shivered. "You could stop and help."

"Not a cop anymore." As soon as he said it, his face eased. "I never thought I'd say that."

A few more turns and the car slowed. The paint job was no longer glossy. Great patches of primer bloomed on the Chevy's sides and hood, and its engine noise had turned choppy, a growl instead of a purr.

Peachtree Apartments, a faded lightbox sign buzzed, whispering a phone number that was probably defunct. The tenement rose, tier upon tier, larger and rougher than Lodi's, starred with rows of small, golden windows. It had once worn a brick facade on the lower levels, now cracked and discolored; higher up, the naked truth of concrete showed.

"This really is a bad neighborhood," Evan muttered. Billowing black bags bulged, stacked along the sidewalks; no few of them had burst and spilled their contents. Pedestrians hurried along, shoulders hunched, quick furtive breaths turning to white clouds.

"Are you afraid?" It didn't seem likely.

A smile tugged at one corner of his mouth. "Not really. You?"

"Maybe." She considered it. "No." If there was magic, there was nothing to fear.

He didn't understand, of course. "Good. I'll take care of you." A no-parking zone, chipped red paint along the kerb, accepted the car without qualm, and a fire hydrant jutted up next to the rear passenger door. "This shouldn't take long. She said we just need to drop it off."

"You think anyone will tow the car?" It was a ridiculous thought, but

"If they do, I'll jack another one." He cut the engine and studied the building, the sidewalk, the bags of trash. "Bring the bag."

Irritation burned behind Cara's eyelids. Of *course* she would bring the bag.

16

Dark, narrow halls redolent of cheap hot food, crowded human breathing, and grease swallowed them. There was no elevator; the stairwells were bare concrete. Once there had been metal balustrades and carpeting, but both had been torn free, by misadventure or for resale. Instead of going up, though, Evan led them *down*. Basement, sub-basement, Evan eyed the broken mechanism on top of a fire door and shook his pale head before ushering her through.

Another hall, this one under buzzing fluorescents and without even the pretense of carpeting, ran for a short while, doors on either side. B211, B212—the doors, each with a brand-new, brass deadlock installed, marched steadily to the very end, where the queen of the hallway sat, regal with all her hardware replaced.

B277.

A shiver poured down her back. The bag was heavy, its strap cutting her sweating palm. Her bare knees felt very exposed, her calves cold.

A wide-shouldered man in a black suit stood in front of

B277, his broad, scarred hands clasped at crotch level. His hair could have been any color, slicked back under a heavy load of grease, and his posture was that of a doorman blessed with a certain amount of bulk but cursed with seeing too many gangster movies. He puffed up as they approached, his gaze locking onto Cara's chest until Evan cleared his throat. Then, the doorman noticed the burlap bag, and his eyes widened. He straightened even further, and a faint sheen appeared on his forehead. By the time they reached speaking distance, he was positively dewy.

"Uh." He cleared his throat. "You're, uh, from *her*?"

"She came herself." Evan indicated Cara, whose throat had closed to a pinhole. Whatever was in the bag had acquired its own gravity, and almost pulled her sideways. The burlap straps sank into her palm, unmercifully.

"Oh. Uh, I thought she was..." The man swallowed whatever he intended to say, and fumbled in his pocket.

Older. He thought I was Lodi. A rancid laugh rose in Cara's throat. Evan glanced at her; she looked down at the bag. The package inside grew even heavier, she swung it in front of her to hold the straps with both hands.

The doorman finally got the locks to work; his hand shook so badly the top one took four tries. "Sorry," he kept muttering, glancing over his shoulder with fear-ringed eyes. The grease in his hair was beginning to melt, and a dropping strand curved across his forehead, an arc of nervousness.

It's all right, Cara wanted to say. Instead, she looked at Evan. "Tell him to calm down."

"Do you think it would help?" His mouth curled in a lazy, cruel line. When he did so, his profile was handsome, but a rasp of disgust slid through her. There was no reason to be cruel.

The doorman hunched his beefy shoulders. "I got it, I got it." Metal clicked and slid aside. "Please, I got it. Sir, ma'am." He pushed it wide and stood aside, waving them forward with frantic little beckoning motions. "See? Please, go on in. Light switch is right there."

Evan preceded her. The doorman's hair-oil was clove-scented; a wave of spice over a sharp mildewy trickle of fear. This close, she could see the shabby, shiny patches on his black suit, and the butt of a gun under his left armpit. She might have tried an encouraging smile, but now he was looking everywhere except at her.

The darkness inside was a living wall of ink until Evan found the light switch. Cara, her steps clicking on concrete, blinked as more fluorescents buzz-guttered into life.

B277 was a long low windowless room, the floor turning to tile near the back end. A metal table stood on the tiles, a drain lingered underneath, exhaling a faint breath of sewage.

"Holy shit," Evan said, softly. "That's Mason Gregory."

The door swung shut behind them, and the man outside must have gotten over his fright, because the locks turned one after another and his footsteps squeak-hurried away, cheap wingtips making tired little noises. They stopped before he reached the end, though, and an electric, humming silence fell.

"He locked us in," Cara whispered.

"It doesn't matter." Evan's was hushed, too. The metal table was actually a gurney, and the shape on it was shrouded and human; a white sheet, folded down, showed the bare iron-haired shoulders of an old man. His blue-lipped face, decorated by a dapper white mustache, was slack and thoughtless. The two livid arms of a Y-incision reached for his shoulders, once neatly mended with black thread. "Mason fucking Gregory. Wow."

The careful stitches had been snipped, and flesh folded aside revealed the meat underneath.

Burlap cut Cara's hands. She glided for the table, impelled. "I can't stop," she whispered, frantically. "Evan? *Evan!*"

"You don't have to." He sounded very certain. "She said you'd know what to do."

"Evan...Evan *no*...no..." Oh, she did. Now that she was here, she knew what was required. Her hands on the corpse, and whatever they would show her.

The thing in the burlap bag began to throb. *Thump. Thump.*

Thump-thump.

Thump-thump.

Thump-thump.

17

IT WAS NO USE. STRUGGLING, A SINGLE DROP OF SWEAT trickling down her spine, Cara was dragged forward. The lump in the bag rolled toward the gurney, a bowling ball on a downhill track. Her arms lifted, because the thing—the horrid, thumping lump—rose, straining at the fabric. It *levitated*, and pulled her resisting body behind it. She tried digging her heels in; they only landed sharply against concrete, tiny guncracks of frustration. When she stepped onto the tile the noise changed. Diamanté buckles glittered angrily, and her shoes, turned traitor, slipped and slithered.

"Cara..." The breath left Evan in a rush. He moved to the door, and she could have told him there was no knob on the inside. The locks were merely round shiny guard-discs on this side, too.

Cara didn't have to look. She *knew*. Just as she knew what the thing in the sack was, and what the soft stealthy noises outside the door meant.

Mason Gregory, whoever he was, had to be attended to. The people outside were for Evan to attend to, and from the sound of it, he was going to need whatever magic Lodi had forced upon them both.

I never forced, the old woman's voice cackled inside Cara's head. Was it real, or just what she *would* say?

The sheet whispered aside. Naked, the middle-aged corpse lay on its back, its gut slightly deflated. Busy hands had been at work, removing organs and weighing them, noting a cause of intimate clockwork stoppage—coronary occlusion and liver toxicity from a chemical pushed secretively through a syringe. Pocked bullet marks, long healed, spattered across the belly as well. Cara's left hand, disregarding the rest of her, plunged into the burlap bag and brought out the wrapped package. It squeezed itself obscenely in her grip, old and vital, and her right hand picked at the butcher's wrapping. Her palms ached, sensitive, and Evan stood at the door, his pale head cocked.

"Shit," he whispered. "We have company. I didn't even know this guy was *dead*."

"Who is he?" she heard herself say, from very far away. A dreamy, disconnected question, because she didn't quite care. Revulsion crawled up her arms, settled behind her breastbone, and she wondered if the mushrooms had merely taken their time to work.

No, she realized. She couldn't be poisoned now. Harmed, certainly, possibly even killed—again—but not *poisoned*.

"Old man Gregory." Evan stood rooted at the door. "Big wheel. He only owns half the rackets in the city."

"Someone poisoned him," she informed him, flatly. "His heart gave out."

"Was that it?" He reached under his jacket as the sheet fell with a whisper. She had to climb atop the rickety gurney, and neither of her hands would uncramp from around the pulsing thing.

"Help me," she whispered. "Please help me. I don't want to."

"Babe, in about five minutes we're gonna have other problems. Whatever you're gonna do, do it *quick*."

"Please." If he would just *listen*. "I don't want to. I can't. Please don't—"

"Just *do it*, so we can get out of here!" Evan swore, and kicked the door again. "Waiting for us outside," he muttered. "God *damn* it." He reached for the light switch.

Terror, wine-red and total, swarmed through Cara's blood. "No. Don't. *No!*"

His hand scythed down, and the darkness came back.

It wasn't just blackness. It was an *absence*, and in its grasp she remembered, for a single vertiginous second, what had happened when the windows blew and aluminum disintegrated, when gravity crushed a fragile winged tube against unforgiving walls of air and later, earth.

We're going to have some turbulence, folks.

The paper in her hands parted. Muscle-gristle throbthudded against her palms, and the squealing thing it had lived in had felt pain and terror before the stun-hammer descended and it was knocked into the absence as well.

Flight 277 to Cincinnati is now boarding.

For a moment, she was so close. The name of the woman boarding that plane, the woman who saw a blonde stewardess's neck-snapped, bloody-tooth smile as the falling shook and snapped and swept them all, trembled on the other side of a diaphanous veil. All she had to do was brush against it, the woven strands would part, and she could go into the absence with that name, falling like a star into the soft forgetful brushing of dark wings.

But the thing in her hands had its own crude force, hammering and battering at her body. It forced her hands to wrench skin and sawn ribs aside, to thrust the lump of gristle-meat into its proper cavity, to twist and jerk the ribs back into their places. Her palms scorched, her fingers cramping, and the *absence* roared, cheated of its natural prey.

Noise. Flashes of sterile white light. Cursing, screaming—bones snapped, and Evan roared, a deathless being in a paroxysm of rage.

That's why there have to be two of us, she realized, dreamily. Her bare knees rested on either side of the body's naked hips; her hands, spattered with effluvia and embalming fluid, clasped cold, loosely boned shoulders. She bent in a grotesque simulacrum of passion, knowing it was necessary but everything in her screaming and turning away from the violation, her body not her own.

Mason Gregory had visited Lodi, too. Cara could *see* the man's bulk in the elevator, his tailored suit enclosing shoulders gone soft from fine living, but his gaze keen and sharp as a scalpel.

You know what I want, he said to Lodi, who cackled in her antique kitchen and drummed her yellowing fingernails on the table.

Yes, the old woman had said. *This time, I'll give it to you.*

Screaming. Seizure locked Cara's traitorous body in position. Energy roared through her into the dumb dense meat beneath, sparking it, drag-harvesting something foul and bleak. Living breath passed from her in a gush, tearing as it left, and that name, the name she wanted, the *other* name, drew close and whispered behind the cheesecloth curtain...

...and fled down into the well of the *absence* as an act of power, complete, nailed its unwilling transmitter in place and the recipient of the act thrashed, jolted back into life.

And consciousness.

18

CARA SPILLED ASIDE. HER HIP LANDED ON TILE WITH stunning, cracking force, her shoulder, the side of her head. Fluorescent tubes shattered, and the white flashes were from gun muzzles.

Evan moved among the men, almost blurring, slapping aside their weapons. An arm broke, a knee kicked and a skull smashed against concrete, the platinum-haired man didn't even need to draw his own gun. He winnowed his opponents, and the sounds they made before his foot came down to break a skull and spatter brainmatter across slick solid greyness echoed against stolid concrete. The hallway, framed by the shattered door and the gurney's stick supports, was a digestive canal, flexing and releasing as it was stuffed with wounded. Each door had opened, disgorging a flood of men in dark suits or jeans and hoodies. Baseball bats, guns, knives—it made no difference. Evan laughed at them, the knives blunted against his fresh new skin, the bullets somehow avoiding him, blunt objects jolting to a stop, reverberating or breaking, meeting a pillar too hard to crush.

The gurney rocked and groaned and the thing on it thrashed. Cara, tossed onto cold tile, tried to close her eyes. They drifted shut, but opened again. The same force that impelled her towards the corpse now refused to let her look away.

The most grievously injured ones fled to the *absence*, that place denied her. She watched them go, and each one whispered the name she wanted so badly to know. If she could only hear, if the rest of them would just be quiet, she could flee as well.

Two pale blobs swung into view. Heels rough with callus, scaled like dinosaur claws, and old-man toenails yellow and not trimmed often enough. Lividity along the back of the calves was disappearing rapidly as the act completed its work, dragging a torn, mended, weighed, measured, embalmed body into the daylight world again.

Now, the sacrifice, Lodi's voice whispered, horrifically gleeful.

Evan shook aside blows, shedding them like rainwater. Only three of the men were left—no, a crack of a neck breaking, and there were two. One was the doorman, on his knees and gibbering in an ecstasy of fear, his hands empty.

The last man was young, tanned, in a grey wool suit, a chunky Rolex on his wrist. His .45 barked at almost point-blank range, and Evan simply paused, smiling rather kindly.

"Curtis," he said, and the name echoed. Somehow the noise of battle had died.

There was nobody left to fight.

"Curtis Gregory," Evan repeated. "You've always been a little shit."

Stunned recognition spread over the young man's face. Evan grabbed at the grey wool lapel, drew his fist back.

"Wait," a gravel-rasping voice said. The snap of

command lay under the word, a man used to being heeded, obeyed.

Evan halted. Surprise lifted his pale eyebrows.

Curtis dropped the gun. It landed on a corpse and vanished into the river of the dead.

"Wait," Mason Gregory repeated. He'd wrapped the sheet around himself, toga-style, and the scaled bottoms of his feet rasped against tile as he took one tentative step, another.

"Daddy..." Curtis moaned. His knees folded; he landed with a crunch on a still-twitching corpse of a man in a Brooks Brothers shirt, red suspenders, pleated trousers, and a neat hole in the center of his forehead from friendly fire.

Cara found she could breathe again. Her head rang, a vast soft brushing of those black feathers. Her own heart kept squeeze-releasing, and that sensation filled her with weary disgust, too.

At least it wasn't the hideous, compelling itch that robbed her of volition.

"Thank you," Mason Gregory husked. "You've done your job. That one's mine."

19

EVAN SHOVED THE GURNEY ASIDE WITH CONTEMPTUOUS EASE. It clattered, wheels locked but momentum forcing them to skid, and smacked into the wall. Little bits broke off, pinging, and hit the ground. "Oh, no," he said, gently, and squatted. "Look at this. Shhh, babe. It's all right."

His hands, spattered and speckled with fresh crimson, reached for her. Cara tried to cringe away. "Don't. Don't touch me." If she had to see the horrible things...feel that pain grating and snapping in her own body...

"Don't be ridiculous." His hands closed on her; he slid an arm under her shoulders and pulled her close, putting a knee down. His jeans were blood-spattered, too, and his knee made a soft tacky-wet sound when it met the floor. "I'm not gonna hurt you. See? It's me. It's not one of them."

Better. Stronger. Faster. Was that what he'd bargained for?

"See?" He cradled her, his chin atop her head. "Nothing's ever gonna hurt you, Cara. We're going to be together a long, long time."

"Daddy," the younger man moaned. He looked a little like John, or maybe it was just the orange hue of tanning beds on pampered but shaven daily skin. His hair flopped weakly.

"Don't you *daddy* me," Mason Gregory said. He bent, creakingly, at a tangle of bodies near the door. His big blunt hands trembled a little, but all in all, he looked remarkably spry for a man recently full of formaldehyde. "You little *shit*. You try to kill your own father, eh?"

Not try, Cara wanted to say. *Succeeded.*

Evan's other arm wormed under her knees. She sagged against him, her hands feeble flutters, trying to push him away.

"It's all right," he repeated. "I'm right here."

"You could have helped me," she whispered. *You could have stopped me,* she meant.

"I am helping you." He leaned in. Closer, closer, his breath mingling with hers.

Her chin fell to the side, avoiding him.

That was how she saw grizzle-headed Mason Gregory lift the gun he'd fished from the river of broken bodies. "My own son," he said. "My own *son*."

No. The cry welled up inside her, but Evan surged upward, and her head lolled. Her chin buried itself in his shoulder, and her shapeless negation mixed with drips and drabs of drying blood, shreds of leather and torn cotton underneath showing slices of pale skin, roughened by use now, no longer soft and baby-innocent.

"Hang on a second." Evan carried her as if she weighed nothing, his arms two muscle-hard bars, hands strangely gentle. Her chin and nose, mashed against bloody cloth and tattered leather, crawled at the nearness.

The old man turned his head slightly, one shoulder dipping. A knot in the sheet kept it mostly about his large frame, but the hem was now draggled with effluvia. It stank down here, too.

Cara suspected there would be a lot of this smell. Shit, blood, and the brass-cartridge reek of death. She pushed her face deeper into Evan's shoulder, and that softened him for a bare instant.

"You got somethin to say?" the old man husked. "Lodi's little friend, huh."

"Nothing to say, Mr Gregory. Just going to take her out of here before you clean house."

The old man scoffed. But he lowered the gun a little.

"Dad." Curtis had his wits back, it seemed. He was still on his knees amid the dead, but he cleared his throat and held his soft manicured hands up, pleadingly. "I don't know what you think...look, I can explain."

"I did what you said." The doorman suddenly spoke up. "I did what you said, Mr Gregory. I brought...oh, God, I brought your body here..." He leaned aside and retched.

Evan paused. "Hold on," he murmured, and his boots crunched and slipped a little as he chose his footing, step by step, carefully down the nightmare hall.

The gun barked once, and the doorman howled. Evan made a short sharp irritated noise.

Mason Gregory sighed. "You brought my body, and a few of your closest friends, right? Because you knew there would be a delivery. How much did he pay you, huh?"

Cara didn't want to look. It was no use, she knew anyway. The doorman clutched at his belly, bright blood welling between his fingertips. He screamed. Evan kept going, slow and terrible, putting each boot down decisively, crushing an arm, a leg, a hand if they happened to be in the way. He paused briefly, lifted a knee, and Cara knew what he was going to do a fraction of a moment before his foot jackhammered down and bone crunch-splattered, a wrapped melon dropped on a hot sidewalk.

The doorman, silenced forever, subsided into twitching nerve-death.

"No," Cara cried out miserably, the sound swallowed by Evan's shoulder, and Curtis moaned, a short, hopeless sound.

"Daddy..." Frantic babbling now, words tripping over each other. "I didn't mean it, I didn't mean it, *she didn't tell me it was poison Daaaddyyyy—*"

Evan kept going. Step-crunch, step-slip. Step-slip, step-tap on bare plain concrete, his heel slipping a little in something too greasy to be blood. The fluorescents buzzed and Curtis began sobbing. Cara squeezed her eyes shut.

"Eh." Mason Gregory spoke again. They were almost at the end of the hall. "Do I know you, blond boy?"

Evan turned his chin slightly. "No, sir," he said, calmly. "No you do not." He pushed at the bullet-riddled door with his shoulder, and carried Cara through.

He began to climb the stairs, one slow, graceful step at a time.

Seven stairs up, another gunshot echoed in the depths of the sub-basement.

Evan kept going.

20

———

Outside, the sleet had turned to struggling snow, the flakes getting bigger and spreading a soft noise-killing blanket. They starred the windshield, gathering in the corners, and it had warmed a little. Just enough to promise more snow, a layer of innocence covering the bags, the concrete, the secrets in basements.

The car was still there. He settled her in the passenger seat, fastened the seat belt, and closed the door. Cara huddled, shaking, numb, and watched the snow collect in corners. Full dark had fallen, thickening in alleys, the sky paradoxically blooming faint orange with reflected electricity.

When he dropped into the driver's seat she winced. There was no parking ticket on the windshield, just the snow. The engine turned over, the headlights flicked on, and the car was a forgettable mid-grade sedan, its door-locks thudding down as it pulled away from a cockeyed, ice-starred fire hydrant.

Evan rested his hands on the wheel. His ring, grimed with blood, no longer gleamed. "Can't wait to clean up," he said, finally, and turned the wipers on. A burst of flakes went by on a flirting wind. "How about you? You okay?"

No. Her hands scrubbed at each other, lifted to her mouth. She wiped at her lips with cold fingers, her teeth threatening to chatter. Warm air soughed through the vents —the engine hadn't even cooled all the way. "You knew them. You knew them *both*."

"Everyone knows them." But his chin settled, and a ghost of the man who had brought her an apple peered from underneath the bleaching. He submerged, and Evan straightened in his seat, touched the accelerator. This new man filled out the broad shoulders, was at home under the blood-spattered jacket. "We're going home."

"That's not home." It was a trap, hungry iron jaws sharpening triangular teeth.

"Still." His grey eyes narrowed. "I know you're tired, but there's one thing left to do."

"Oh, I know." The knowledge was there, whole and terrible, under the surface of the world. It took no special sight to touch its shape, run her mental fingers over its hills and valleys. "She'll let us in. You'll stand behind me, and you'll hold my arms while she does what she wants."

And she'll be young again. It was the only possible way this could end. Lodi might be old, and tired...but she had done this before. The same sure, clear instinct that had impelled Cara out of the airport, told her to play dumb, and opened the space for the terrible act of resurrection to come through her knew, and that was enough.

The car rocked a little as he braked again. Evan's knuckles were white. The snowflakes thickened, solidified.

"It's all right," Cara said. "I don't mind. I don't want to do...things like this. I want to go on. I shouldn't be here." *You two deserve each other.* "You gave Curtis the poison, didn't you. For her."

"A lot had to get done." He exhaled, hard. "Is that what she's thinking? That I'm just gonna stand there, and..."

"Evan." Cara turned her chin, gazed sightlessly out the window. "I want you to do it."

"Well, good for you." He scowled at ruby brake lights, tires crunching through fresh snow. In a little while, all the tracks would vanish. "Because I like this new body, and I don't wanna go back to the old one."

PART III

MUNDI FINIS

21

____

He pressed the button, again. The gate looked the same, except its razor edges scalloped with frost. The snow had thickened, it would come down all night. Tomorrow there would be a blank page, and nobody could ever resist spoiling one of those. Anything new was made to be marred.

Lodi must have been waiting. "...Yes?"

"We're back." Evan sounded tired, but his shoulders were iron-hard under his knifed, shot, torn coat. His jeans had dried; flakes of blood cracked and scattered.

The gate buzzed. "Come in."

Stepping over the garden's threshold, the cold fell away. Summer enfolded them, the snow-silence cloven by plaintive cricketsong. A frog croaked, lonesome, held in a luxurious green prison. The plain metal door opened, and Lodi's lair swallowed them both.

Wooden floor, solid and real. Rich golden light. Unexpected beauty stung Cara's eyes. It was quiet and clean here, and the horrid things lying under the surface of the world had retreated.

Evan held the elevator door, reaching over Cara's shoulder. His silence, like his scowl, deepened.

Lodi, rat-haired and sheathed in vivid polyester, lingered bloodshot at her apartment door, peering blearily into the hall. She stamped and huffed with impatience, but a small mischievous chuckle escaped when she saw the state of Evan's clothing. "There you are. Worried an old woman to death, you did. Well?"

"Package is delivered and loose ends cleaned up." Evan delivered the sentence in a monotone. He crowded behind Cara, pushing her through the door. Now his heat was no comfort, but a trap all its own.

Lodi's teeth protruded, gleaming. She smacked her thin lips. "Good, good. And did she speak to anyone but you? Anyone at all?"

"No." Irritation invaded the word. "Of course not."

"Good little girl. And a good little boy. Good children for Mama Lodi. Close the door."

Cara stopped in the hallway, just out of reach. Lodi's teeth bared. Her right hand, held low, was full of a wicked gleam. The old woman, irritated, glanced over Cara's shoulder at Evan, her head craning atop her bent spine. "Close the *door*, idiot."

The heavy wooden door slammed, rattling the frame, the hall, the floor. Light fixtures danced uneasily, and a shadow passed through the hall. Cara closed her eyes.

"Look at this. A tired girl." Lodi shuffled forward. "You. Stand behind her. Hold her shoulders."

"Here?" He was still warm, at least. Even if it was the final trap, he was solid. There were worse ways to go, like disintegrating in an aluminum tube. She waited for the absence to come. It would probably hurt a little, but then it would be—

"What are you *doing*?" Lodi sounded alarmed.

"This."

The gunshot deafened Cara. She swayed—he'd kept his hand low, his arm along her side, and the jolt of recoil passed through his flesh into hers. Her eyelids flew open, and Lodi, lips pulled back and yellowed teeth champing, surged forward. The knife was an icicle blade, lifted high, and next would come its descent, plunging, cleaving, cutting, loosening.

Evan pushed Cara aside. She staggered, her shoulder and hip giving twin barks of muted pain, still bruise-tender from falling from the gurney. The gun spoke again, and Lodi staggered too. Grimly determined, the old woman stabbed at Cara, the blade cleaving air with a low sweet whoosh.

A third shot. Cara's head rang. The name behind the gossamer curtain plucked at her fingers, her toes, at every secret string inside her bones.

"*No!*" the old woman howled. "Noooooo!"

"Yes," Evan said grimly. The knife clattered on hardwood, he kicked it away. Cara strained to remember her old name, to hear it through the noise.

A pop. A showering of wet salt. Lodi's body, twisting and jerking, folded inward, desiccating in fast-forward. Her eyes sank into the sockets, skin thinning and stretching papery over bird-bones. Great rivers ploughed the paper surface, and behind them dust swirled, reeking of cinnamon and natron. Her housedress tore as she kicked and dry-screamed.

It wasn't the bullets, Cara realized. It was Evan's refusal to play along that tore Lodi's grasp on the world free. Refusal, an apple, and a name chosen almost at random.

The mummified skeleton's hand jerked out. Two bone-fingers pointed at Evan; his large hands flew to his own throat and he dropped to his knees with a jolt that shook the entire structure, echoing through unused apartments, swaying the elevator in its cage, puffing dust from ceilings and corners. His paleness purpled, he struggled to inhale.

A coughing, rasping croak spiraled up and up. The housedress collapsed. Granules split, split again, working themselves finer and finer until some unimaginable threshold was crossed, and the pile of dust began to suck in on itself. A whoosh, another gout of dry-mummy desert death, a hot wind through the hall, and a *pop* of air collapsing inward.

Cara leaned against the wall, muscle and bone full of soretooth throbbing. The apartment shivered, touching its new mistress; the floor groaned, the walls shimmered, sensing her. Learning. The entire kitchen rattled, appliances stretching, waking briefly from the slumber of humming electrical servitude to take new shapes. The bedrooms exhaled fresh air and sun-warmed linen. The windows rippled—what would they show her, those glassy eyes?

Evan collapsed onto hands and knees. He whooped in a breath, coughed. The polyester housedress shrank with a soft tearing whisper, a rag of much-bleached, much-washed cloth shredding itself.

Cara peeled herself away from the wall. She stepped out of her shoes, sighing with relief as her calves relaxed. The floor was cool and hard, but no grit touched her sensitive soles. She lowered herself slowly, gently, almost like an elderly woman, and put her arm around Evan. He coughed, sputtered, and the name she longed to hear retreated.

Lodi had probably known it, might even have whispered it as she killed the doll she had crafted so carefully.

The knife was close. She could probably lunge for it. She could even softly, stealthily reach. Close her fingers around its wooden hilt. The glassy blade was hungry. Had it been brought to Lodi in exchange for information?

If she touched it, she would know.

"It's all right," Cara said. The words, dry, stuck in her throat. She patted Evan's back, the ruin of his leather jacket. "It's all right."

"Cara," he rasped. Muscle flexed under leather, fabric, skin. "*Cara.*" To him, that *was* her name.

She leaned close, her black hair against platinum. Her fingertips brushed a wooden hilt—lovingly polished, the glass blade honed to a whisper. Evan shook, and if she was to escape him, too, there would never be a better time.

Snow continued to fall, closing around an apartment building few entered and even fewer left. In the courtyard, the frog, deciding it was useless, set to hunting instead of singing and the leaves moved uneasily, sensing winter outside their snug, soft, loamy home.

finis

ABOUT THE AUTHOR

Lili Saintcrow was born in New Mexico and spent her childhood bouncing around the world as a military brat. She currently resides in the rainy Pacific Northwest with her children, dog, cat, and assorted other strays.